Five Nights at Freddy's™

ESCAPE THE PIZZAPLEX

AN INTERACTIVE NOVEL

BY

SCOTT CAWTHON

LYNDSAY ELY

SCHOLASTIC INC.

Special thanks to DJ Sterf

ISBN 978-93-5954-004-7

This reprint edition June 2025

Book design by Jeff Shake

Printed in India at Shivam Offset Press, New Delhi

Intro

You are Cassie, a kindhearted and adventurous young patron of Freddy Fazbear's Mega Pizzaplex, and human best friend of Gregory, a precocious boy with a penchant for getting into trouble. Lately, you and Gregory have taken to hiding in the Pizzaplex after hours in order to play once everyone else has left. You enjoy the animatronics more than you like most other kids your age, especially Roxanne "Roxy" Wolf, who has been your idol ever since she came to the rescue of your birthday party (that no one showed up to) and made it the best birthday you ever had!

Like Gregory, you have a fondness (and aptitude) for computers and have an intimate understanding of the Pizzaplex and its workings, thanks to your father's work as a Faz-Technician. This means you and Gregory know exactly how to take advantage of all the fun options the Pizzaplex has to offer at night. Sure, it gets a little weird, once all the people are gone and only the animatronics and bots are left, but *weird* is just another term for *cool*, right? Be careful, though—security has gotten much tighter lately due to Gregory's mischief. Management has splurged on renovations along with adding keypads and intercoms.

Tonight, Gregory says he has a special idea for what to do but insists that it has to be a surprise. Which you're willing to go along with . . . you think. As much as you enjoy your time in the Pizzaplex with Gregory, he can be known to take things a little far sometimes.

Still, you wouldn't want him to think you're not up for whatever plans he has in mind. As Gregory's games play out, you'll have many choices to make, which will lead to various outcomes. If you find an item that might help you during the night, write it down for later on the pages provided. But first, you have an important decision to make . . .

- **IF YOU WANT TO PLAY ON *EASY* DIFFICULTY, ADD FLASHLIGHT, BONNIE KEY CHAIN, AND FOOD SERVICE KEY CARD TO YOUR INVENTORY AND TURN TO PAGE 3.**
- **IF YOU WANT TO PLAY ON *NORMAL* DIFFICULTY, START OUT WITH ONLY YOUR WITS AND TURN TO PAGE 3.**

SHORTCUTS:

NIGHT 1

It's finally closing time at Freddy Fazbear's Mega Pizzaplex. Shrouded behind a thick pillar in a dark corner, you and Gregory hide and wait for the last of the Pizzaplex patrons to trickle out the front entrance. After a while, the last of the families leave, carrying their arcade prizes and half-empty plastic souvenir cups, and the heavy door snaps shut, locking after them. A few cleaning bots appear, sweeping through to gather up all the dropped popcorn and discarded candy wrappers as the lights dim, leaving only the neon signs to cast their sharp, vivid glow across the main lobby. It gets quiet—so quiet you can hear the faint buzz of those lights, and Gregory's breathing where he hides beside you.

"Everyone's gone," Gregory finally says. "Let's go!"

He moves deliberately but silently—there are still security bots roaming around, after all—and you follow, staying close and keeping an eye out as you cross the lobby and head for the stairs that lead up to the mainstage area. You pass the giant Freddy fountain at the lobby center, being careful as you travel, but by now, the two of you know what to expect, and how to avoid discovery. A few bots aren't going to stop you. At night, the Pizzaplex becomes *your* playground.

And what a playground it is! Even when empty, there's a busy energy to the space. It's like there's a song playing, something you can't quite make out, but one that never stops, even at night. Not that you can really tell that it's night. Other than the lowered lights, the Pizzaplex feels almost the same at night as it does during the day.

Almost.

➤ **TURN TO PAGE 4.**

Gregory moves like he has a plan already, though he didn't bother to mention anything earlier while you both were waiting for everyone to leave. But at this point in your friendship, you can tell when he's got an idea in mind. If only he'd give you a hint or two.

"Where are we headed?" you ask.

"Shhh," he says, but gestures for you to keep following.

You realize your destination soon enough. Heading past the main-stage, you enter the hall where the mascots, the Glamrock Animatronics, have their greenrooms. They run in a line, first Freddy's, then Roxy's, then Monty's, and, finally, Chica's. Roxy is your favorite, but Gregory leads you into Freddy's greenroom, where Freddy is standing in the corner. From the way Gregory runs over to him, it's clear Freddy has been waiting. The animatronic comes to life as you approach, eyes going bright and a wide smile stretching across his face.

"Hello, Gregory," Freddy says happily. "Hello, Cassie. Are you ready to play the game?"

"Game?" you say. "What game?"

Gregory turns back to you with a mischievous twinkle in his eye. "Tonight we're going to play hide-and-seek. You and I are going to hide, and Freddy's going to seek."

"Ooh, okay." You were a little worried about what Gregory had in mind, but hide-and-seek is simple enough, and it even sounds like fun. "What are the rules?"

"Pffft," Gregory says. "We don't need rules. We can hide anywhere in the Pizzaplex. But the first one to get found by Freddy loses!"

"Wait," says Freddy, holding up a finger. "Don't forget, Gregory. There *is* one rule. You both get a head start before I start looking for you."

➤ TURN TO PAGE 5.

A head start sounds reasonable enough, though Freddy doesn't elaborate on how long you have to hide.

"When do we start?" you ask.

Gregory smiles. "Now!" he cries, and dashes off before you can protest.

You pout and cross your arms. Typical Gregory. Not outright cheating, but he certainly could have given you more warning!

"Time is ticking," Freddy says. You don't waste another moment. You run off, but by the time you get into the hallway outside the greenroom, Gregory is long gone. You take a few more steps, then slow, unsure which way to go. After all, the Pizzaplex is HUGE. The Superstar Daycare, Chica's Mazercise, the Prize Counter . . . there are so many places you can think of to hide that you don't know where to start! The hallway leads off in opposite directions, so picking which way to go would be a good start. Your gaze is also drawn to the door to Roxy's greenroom, which is a short walk away, and open. Roxanne Wolf—with her wild silver hair and edgy punk-rock style—is your idol.

You can still remember how sad you felt when you had your birthday party at the Pizzaplex and none of the kids you invited showed up. It was Roxy who came to your rescue, singing and dancing and making sure you had fun. Because of her, it turned out to be the best birthday ever, and Roxy has been your favorite member of the Glamrock Animatronics ever since.

You know the Pizzaplex like the back of your hand, but if anyone would know a good place to hide where Freddy wouldn't think to look, it would be Roxy. The door to Monty's greenroom is also open, and something sitting just inside catches your eye. You can't quite make it out, but whatever it is, it's not something you've seen in the Pizzaplex before. Maybe you should check it out?

You think for a few moments, considering your options. But Freddy's generous head start is already ticking down, so there's no time to waste!

- IF YOU WANT TO TURN LEFT DOWN THE HALLWAY, TURN TO PAGE 7.
- IF YOU WANT TO TURN RIGHT DOWN THE HALLWAY, TURN TO PAGE 8.
- IF YOU WANT TO GO INTO ROXY'S GREENROOM AND TALK TO HER, TURN TO PAGE 9.
- IF YOU WANT TO GO INTO MONTY'S GREENROOM AND INVESTIGATE THE MYSTERY ITEM, TURN TO PAGE 10.

You finally decide to take a left down the hallway and head back into the atrium of the Pizzaplex. There, you go to the top of the escalators and pause. There are so many places to hide, you need to take another moment to think. Where is Freddy least likely to search? You look around and see the entrance to the Superstar-cade. The bright pink-and-yellow sign jumps out, beckoning you inside. You consider it for a few more moments, but the Superstar-cade seems as good a place as any to hide in, so you head toward it.

You pass through the entrance, still making sure to avoid any cleaning or security bots that might be roaming around. Inside, the Superstar-cade is a sprawling room, filled with arcade games of all kinds, both lining the walls and set in circular clusters on the red-and-yellow checkered floor. The games are still on at night, and you and Gregory love playing them when no one else is here. Unlike during the day, you never have to wait for the good games to be free!

Unfortunately, you don't see many good places to hide in the arcade other than some photo booths, which give you the creeps. Wandering around, you search everywhere, considering your options. You could try wedging yourself behind one of the game cases, but that looks like it would be a tight fit. There's also a bathroom. Maybe that would be a better idea. After all, there are a *lot* of bathrooms in the Pizzaplex. Freddy might not bother to search them all.

"Tick-tock, tick-tock." Suddenly, you hear Freddy's booming voice. "Time is up, kids. Ready or not, here I come!"

Your heart starts to pound. You have to make a decision, and quick!

➤ IF YOU HIDE BEHIND AN ARCADE CABINET, TURN TO PAGE 11.

➤ IF YOU RUN INTO THE BATHROOM TO HIDE, TURN TO PAGE 13.

After some thought, you decide to take a right down the hallway and head back into the Pizzaplex atrium. There, you pause to think again. There are so many areas to choose from, any one of which might be a good hiding spot, and it's hard to decide where Freddy will be the least likely to look for you. A part of you still wants to look for Roxy and ask her opinion, but you don't want to turn back now. You've wasted enough of your head start as it is. But thinking of Roxy gives you a great idea: You're going to hide in Roxy Raceway! The neon purple-drenched go-kart track is one of your favorite places to hang out at the Pizzaplex, mostly since it's Roxy's area. But with all the cars and garages and such, there are plenty of places there where you can avoid Freddy. Hopefully, Gregory hasn't had the same idea!

You head into Roxy Raceway, making your way through the reception area. Like before, you're almost overwhelmed by the choices available to you. You could stay close to the entrance and find a hiding spot in the reception area. Or you could head down into the racetrack area, where there are go-karts and garages and more.

What would Roxy do?

You stand at the rail, considering your options for so long that you jump a little when you hear Freddy's booming voice.

"Time's up!" he says excitedly. "Ready or not, here I come!"

You frown. If Freddy finds you before you've even gotten a chance to hide, Gregory will tease you all night. You need to be ready, and quick!

- **IF YOU WANT TO HIDE IN THE RECEPTION AREA, TURN TO PAGE 26.**
- **IF YOU WANT TO HEAD INTO THE RACEWAY TO HIDE IN ONE OF THE GO-KARTS, TURN TO PAGE 27.**
- **IF YOU WANT TO HIDE IN ONE OF THE RACEWAY GARAGES, TURN TO PAGE 28.**

Freddy Fazbear is an animatronic. And to outsmart an animatronic in a game of hide-and-seek, you decide you need to get help from another animatronic! Plus, you always like a reason to visit Roxy. You run to the open door of her greenroom and go inside. As always, it's aglow in awesome neon green and purple light, with white-and-black checkerboard flags and tires from Roxy Raceway decorating the walls. It's so cool, you wish you had a room just like it.

But the one thing missing from this awesome space is Roxy.

"Roxy? Are you here? It's me, Cassie."

You step farther inside and look around, but your favorite rockstar is nowhere to be seen . . . which is strange. After operating hours, the Glamrock Animatronics usually return to their greenrooms until it's time for the Pizzaplex to reopen in the morning. Maybe Roxy is in the Rehearsal Room? Or deeper in the bowels of the Pizzaplex, getting maintenance done?

You want to continue searching for Roxy, to figure out where she might have gone. Unfortunately, you don't have time, and you've already wasted enough of your head start. You need to take a different direction if you're going to find a good hiding place and evade Freddy longer than Gregory does. There's no way you can let him win—you'll never hear the end of it! You leave Roxy's greenroom, heading back to where you came from.

- **IF YOU WANT TO TURN LEFT DOWN THE HALLWAY, TURN TO PAGE 7.**
- **IF YOU WANT TO TURN RIGHT DOWN THE HALLWAY, TURN TO PAGE 8.**
- **IF YOU HAVEN'T VISITED MONTY'S GREENROOM YET TO INVESTIGATE THE MYSTERY ITEM AND WANT TO, TURN TO PAGE 10.**

You decide to head down the hall to Monty Gator's greenroom and check out the strange item. But as curious as you are, you move cautiously. Of all the animatronics and bots in the Pizzaplex, Monty is the one who creeps you out the most, though you're not sure why. It's probably just because of his big alligator claws. Or maybe it's his teeth.

His many, MANY teeth.

Still, that apprehension doesn't stop you from investigating what it is that you spy through his open doorway. You pause just inside the greenroom, which, more than the other greenrooms, is literally the greenest. Giant stars light up the emerald walls, illuminating the images of Monty that decorate them. There are some leaves growing in the corners, which gives the room a vaguely tropical feel, but you're pretty sure they're plastic. Oddly, Monty isn't anywhere around. But maybe he's getting maintenance done before the Pizzaplex reopens in the morning.

Regardless, you didn't come here looking for Monty. There, a few steps away, is the thing you spied through the doorway: a crate. A sleek, brand-new crate. It's not small, but it's not as big as some of the storage crates you've seen in other parts of the Pizzaplex, either. What could be in there? A new decoration for the walls? Maybe an upgraded instrument?

You move closer, your curiosity getting the best of you. You've never been good at ignoring a mystery. But when you try to open the crate, the lock flashes red at you. You fiddle with it for a few seconds, but Freddy's head start is ticking away, and you don't have time to waste. And from what you can tell, only a key card is going to solve the mystery of whatever this crate contains.

- **IF YOU WANT TO GO BACK TO WHERE YOU CAME FROM AND TURN LEFT DOWN THE HALLWAY, TURN TO PAGE 7.**
- **IF YOU WANT TO GO BACK TO WHERE YOU CAME FROM AND TURN RIGHT DOWN THE HALLWAY, TURN TO PAGE 8.**
- **IF YOU HAVEN'T VISITED ROXY'S GREENROOM YET AND WANT TO, TURN TO PAGE 9.**

You decide Freddy will be least likely to find you if you hide behind one of the arcade cabinets. There's one up against a wall that has a small gap behind it, just wide enough for you to fit behind. You wiggle into the space, which is actually pretty decent, as far as hiding places go. Then you look down. There's a vent in the wall, with a cover that's slightly askew. You give it a nudge with your foot and it comes off, revealing a crawlspace. You smile at your good fortune. Now that's a much better hiding spot! No way Freddy would think to look for you in there.

Carefully, you crouch down and crawl inside. It's so dark you can barely see, but just inside the vent your hand suddenly brushes against something cylindrical and metallic. You fumble for it, finally lifting it close enough to your face to make out what it is. It's a flashlight! One of the Faz-Technicians must have left it in the vent while doing maintenance. Definitely something that could come in handy later. You shove the flashlight into your bag, then curl up to wait, imagining where Gregory is hiding. Wherever it is, there's no way it's as good as this spot.

After a while, you hear something approaching. Then, a voice calling out.

"Grreeegggorrry . . . Caaassssiiieeee . . ." It's Freddy. "Where are youuuuu?"

You smile to yourself. It doesn't matter that Freddy thought to look for you in the Superstar-cade—he'll never find you in the vent!

Crash!

You nearly jump as a loud noise startles you. Another follows it. And another.

Your stomach twists into a knot. Is this part of the game? If so, it's not like any game of hide-and-seek you've ever played before. Nervous and curious, you risk a look outside the vent. With the game in the way, you can only see a thin sliver of the Superstar-cade, but as you watch, another arcade cabinet crashes to the floor.

"Gregory! Cassie!" Freddy speaks more sharply this time. "WHERE ARE YOU?"

What is wrong with Freddy? You recoil as the animatronic overturns more games. This can't be right. Freddy is definitely taking the game way too seriously. And worse, if he overturns the game in front of your vent, maybe he'll decide to search behind it. You glance down the passage. Maybe going deeper would be safer, just in case. Then again, maybe you should find Gregory. He's sure to know what's going on with Freddy!

- **ADD FLASHLIGHT TO YOUR INVENTORY. IF YOU GO DEEPER INTO THE VENT, TURN TO PAGE 14.**
- **ADD FLASHLIGHT TO YOUR INVENTORY. IF YOU LEAVE THE VENT TO GO FIND GREGORY, TURN TO PAGE 15.**

After considering your options, you finally decide to hide in the bathroom. After all, who wants to willingly spend lots of time in a bathroom? Freddy will never think to look for you there. You run across the Superstar-cade to the corner where the bathrooms are, where you think for a moment before throwing open the door to the women's restroom. Inside, the fluorescent lights flicker weakly, and one of the faucets is dripping, the *plunk plunk plunk* in time with your steps as you move deeper into the restroom. To top it off, there is a damp, vaguely unpleasant smell, like water that has been standing too long.

You start to regret choosing this as a hiding spot. Certainly there are cleaner, brighter, and less smelly spots in the Superstar-cade. But there's no time to turn back. Freddy could come into the arcade looking for you at any moment!

There are three stalls that you can hide in, all the same electric shade of pink. The color's the only thing that brightens the room up. You consider them for a moment. If you hide inside and stand on the toilet so your feet aren't visible, you should be safe! But which one do you choose?

➤ IF YOU WANT TO HIDE IN STALL #1, TURN TO PAGE 16.

➤ IF YOU WANT TO HIDE IN STALL #2, TURN TO PAGE 18.

➤ IF YOU WANT TO HIDE IN STALL #3, TURN TO PAGE 19.

Freddy's voice continues to grow louder and the crashing continues, leaving you with a strange feeling in the pit of your stomach. You decide it would be a bad idea to leave the vent now. Whatever is going on with Freddy, you'd rather wait for him to move on before you try to look for Gregory. And to stay safe, you decide *deeper* in the vent would be better. Maybe if you're lucky, you can find another vent to exit out of, somewhere far from Freddy.

You shimmy farther down the passageway, crawling on your hands and knees, trying to stay as quiet as possible. It isn't easy in this tight space, so you move carefully, until you come across another discarded item. Picking it up, you peer closely at it. It's a piece of chewy candy. Must have been a very careless Faz-Technician to leave all their stuff behind. But it's your candy now.

You put it in your bag, then continue making your way into the depths of the Pizzaplex, away from the Superstar-cade. But in your haste, your hand slips. Before you can catch yourself, your elbow knocks against the wall of the vent with a loud, metallic *clang*!

You freeze. Was that as loud outside the vent as it sounded inside? Your heart starts to throb in your ears, and the air turns thick, making it difficult to breathe.

Did Freddy hear you?

➤ ADD TEETHY CHEW TO YOUR INVENTORY AND TURN TO PAGE 20.

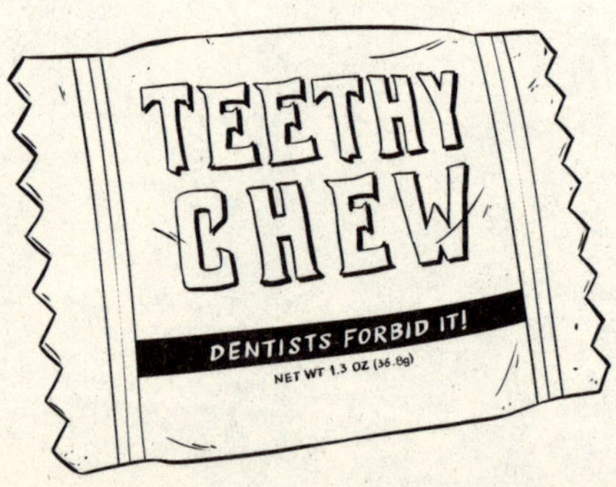

You don't like the way Freddy sounds as he searches for you. Something seems to be wrong with him, given what he's doing to the video games. Maybe he's simply taking the "seek" part of hide-and-seek too seriously, but you're not willing to risk that. And if anyone would be able to figure out why Freddy is acting the way he is, it would be Gregory. You need to find your friend before Freddy finds you.

This means you need to leave the vent. This is easier said than done, though, with Freddy right outside somewhere, lurking in the arcade. Moving to the opening of the passage, you peek out into the dark, but you can't see much from your vantage point. Instead, you listen closely for Freddy. The banging has stopped and you can no longer hear him calling for you, but you're not sure what that means. Maybe he's moved on to another part of the Pizzaplex—that's what you hope, at least. Regardless, you can't see him, and if you move fast, you should be able to escape from the Superstar-cade before Freddy spots you.

Moving as quietly as you can, you climb out of the vent, then creep around the edge of the game case.

Suddenly, Freddy steps into view.

➤ **TURN TO PAGE 22.**

Stall #1 is the closest, so you run to it, closing the door after you. Being careful not to slip, you climb up on the toilet cover. It's even darker in here. The lights directly overhead have burned out, and no one has replaced the bulbs. Beyond the door, the working lights continue to flicker, a faint fizzing sound accompanying each flash. Definitely not the cheeriest spot in the Pizzaplex. You crouch and start to wait, trying to stay as small and unnoticeable as possible. With any luck, wherever Gregory has chosen to hide will be more obvious, and Freddy will find him first.

That hope grows the longer you crouch, even as your legs begin to ache from awkwardly huddling on the toilet. Every few minutes you stand up to let them stretch, taking the chance to look over the edge of the stall and across the bathroom, to the exit door. There's nothing to see, of course.

Then, suddenly, you hear noises from beyond the door. But they're strange and, at first, you can't tell what they are. Something heavy is falling. Once. Twice. Then, there's a sound like glass breaking.

"Greeeggoorryyy . . ." It's Freddy's voice. He's in the Superstar-cade! "Caassssiiiiieee . . ." But Freddy sounds weird. Not as cheery as he did when you began the night. "Come out, come out, wherever you are!"

Is this part of the game? There's another crash, and you start to have a sinking feeling that no, no it's not.

"Where are you?!" Freddy roars in the distance.

Your skin turns cold. Something is wrong. Something is *terribly* wrong with Freddy. You remain still, not sure what to do. If Gregory were here, maybe he could do something. Talk to Freddy. Check his programming. But Freddy doesn't listen to you the way he listens to Gregory, and you don't have anything to interface the animatronic with. It's obvious what you need to do now: find Gregory.

And hope that Freddy doesn't find him first.

You shift slightly, straining to hear what's happing outside in the Superstar-cade. The noises have disappeared, which is encouraging. If

Freddy has given up and moved on, that will give you the chance to slip out and go look for Gregory.

Bam!

The bathroom door slams open.

➤ **TURN TO PAGE 23.**

You decide on the middle stall of the three, going over to it and pushing the door open. It's looser than you realize, banging against the side of the stall loud enough to make you wince. You glance back over your shoulder, hoping no one—especially Freddy—heard that, but after a few moments, all you hear is silence. You go inside Stall #2 and close the door behind you, trying to slide the lock into place. But it comes loose. You try it again, but it's no good. The lock is busted. And without it, the door won't stay shut. If Freddy comes in, he'll spot you in a heartbeat!

Maybe you can wedge the door shut. You push it back into place, fishing around your pockets and bag for something to shove into the gap near the hinge. Something that will keep it from swinging back open.

Then, beyond the door to the bathroom, you hear something. A voice calling.

"Where are youuuuuu?" It's Freddy. But he sounds . . . off. Not like his usual self. Certainly not as cheery as he did at the start of the night. "Gregoryyyyy! Cassieeeee! *Where are you?*"

You freeze. The last three words come as an angry, snappish snarl. What in the world is wrong with Freddy?

And, more importantly, how much noise were you making when trying to keep the door shut?

Despite your efforts, the door isn't going to remain shut. You let go, allowing the door to fall open, then start for one of the other stalls. You can only hope that their locks work, and that Freddy didn't hear you in here, messing around with the broken stall door.

Suddenly, before you have the chance to hide, the door to the bathroom flies open. Freddy's shadowy form fills the entry, his eyes aglow in a way that make your knees feel weak.

He looks right at you and snarls.

➤ TURN TO PAGE 25.

You head to hide in the last stall in the row, thinking the farthest one will make the best place to hide. Stall #3 it is. But the moment you open the door, your heart drops, and you know that this choice is the wrong one. The toilet seat is missing, which means you won't be able to crouch on it so that no one spots your feet under the stall door. And there's no other way to obscure yourself in the narrow space.

You begin to turn away, to choose another stall, when a glimmer of light catches your eye. Next to the toilet, someone has dropped a hair clip, glittery pink and covered with rhinestones. It's cool enough that you ignore the fact that it's on a bathroom floor and pick it up, adding it to your bag.

Then, you go to pick a different stall.

- **ADD HAIR CLIP TO YOUR INVENTORY. IF YOU WANT TO HIDE IN STALL #1, TURN TO PAGE 16.**
- **ADD HAIR CLIP TO YOUR INVENTORY. IF YOU WANT TO HIDE IN STALL #2, TURN TO PAGE 18.**

You wait for what seems like forever, but you don't hear anything outside the vent.

Then, you take a deep breath and let it out.

Suddenly, back at the opening of the vent, there's a loud *crash*. More light fills the space, but only for a moment before a dark form blocks it out.

"I found you!" cries Freddy, laughing maniacally. "I found you!"

His face fills the whole of the opening, his robotic eyes wide. You don't like the look on his face—it's too bright and too angry at the same time. You don't know what's going on, but this isn't the Freddy that began the game with you. His face disappears and is replaced by a hand, which reaches out for you, grabbing at the air. You scramble, trying to get away, but you only make it a little farther down the vent before something blocks your progress. It's a grate. In the low light earlier, you never saw it.

You're trapped.

"I found you!" Freddy cries again and again. He lunges, hand closing around your ankle painfully. He yanks you out of the vent, onto the floor of the Superstar-cade.

"I found you!" Freddy looms above you now, scowling, his eyes wild in a way that makes your blood run cold. Something is very, very wrong with him. "You lose!"

Freddy reaches for you again.

You scream.

Suddenly, Freddy's chest opens up and Gregory bursts out, laughing hysterically.

"Wh-what?" You don't understand.

Gregory starts to say something, then stops, laughter overtaking him again. Freddy, now looking normal, chuckles with him.

"I got you!" Gregory finally blurts out between giggles. "Look how scared you were!"

It's only then that you understand: it was all a prank.

"Oh." You blush, smiling a little, even though you don't feel like it.

You were really scared, thinking Freddy was going to hurt you. Still, now that you know it was only one of Gregory's jokes, you feel a little silly. Maybe even embarrassed. "Yeah. I guess you got me."

"See?" Gregory says. "I told you it would be a great game."

Still forcing a smile onto your lips, you nod. You don't really agree, but you also don't want Gregory to think you're no fun.

"Just wait"—Gregory smirks, that mischievous look from earlier back in his eyes—"until you find out what I have in mind for tomorrow!"

➤ **TURN TO PAGE 48.**

At first, Freddy simply stares down at you, frowning. His eyes look weird. Almost . . . wild.

"I found you." He says it quieter than before, in a way that makes a cold shiver run down your spine. "You lose."

Then, he reaches for you. You scramble backward, trying to escape, but his hands clamp around your shoulders, fingers digging in as he lifts you off the ground and pulls you close to his face.

"You lose," he says again.

Unable to hold the fear in any longer, you scream.

Suddenly, Freddy drops you. A moment later, his chest opens up and Gregory bursts out, laughing hysterically.

"Gregory?" You frown, confused. "What's going on?"

But Gregory is laughing too hard to answer. Freddy laughs with him, no longer looking angry or dangerous. Now he looks like his normal, cheerful animatronic self.

"I got you!" Gregory says finally. "I can't believe you fell for that. You were so scared!"

You blush. "What?"

"It was a joke," Gregory says. "And I got you! Wasn't that great?"

You chuckle a little, not really amused. "Oh, uh . . . yeah." You don't want Gregory to think you're a stick in the mud, but it's clear that the prank was funnier to him than it was to you.

"Just wait . . ." Gregory grins. "Tomorrow night we're going to have even *more* fun!"

➤ **TURN TO PAGE 48.**

"Come out, come out . . ." Freddy's voice is low, almost a growl.

In the stall, your fingers tighten, clawing into your legs. If you'd heard him coming sooner, maybe you could have run. But now, all you can think is: you're trapped.

Freddy lurches into the bathroom, each step heavy and sharp against the tile floor. Through the cracks in the stall walls, you see his form pass by. He doesn't stop.

". . . wherever you are."

Then, you hear Freddy pause. In the resulting silence, you hold your breath, your heart pounding. There are faint sounds of movement as if Freddy is searching the bathroom.

"Hm," Freddy says faintly. Then again, sounding more intense this time. *"Hm."*

You bite the inside of your lip. Is he satisfied? Will he move on to search somewhere else in the Pizzaplex?

The cracks in the stall wall darken again as Freddy's form steps in front of the stall. A whimper escapes you.

Slowly, the stall door creaks open, revealing Freddy. His teeth are bared, eyes wild.

"Found you," he growls. There's no time to understand what's happened, or to try to reason with him, before he reaches for you.

You clamp your eyes shut and scream.

Then: laughter.

When you open your eyes again, Freddy's chest is open, revealing Gregory within. Your friend is grinning from ear to ear.

"What . . . ?" You don't understand.

"Got you!" Gregory announces, and starts laughing again. "A toilet? Well, at least you were in the right place in case you peed your pants!"

You blush, understanding now. It was all a joke. One of Gregory's famous pranks.

"Wasn't that a fun game?" Gregory asks.

You chuckle a little, not sure it was. But Gregory tricked you, you have to admit. And you don't want to be a sore loser.

"Hah, yeah, sure," you say, secretly hoping that tomorrow night is less of this kind of "fun."

➤ TURN TO PAGE 48.

Freddy stands in the door of the bathroom, looking wild.

You swallow, your mouth dry. "Ha ha, Freddy . . ." It's hard to talk, but you manage to get the words out. "You found me. Guess I lose!"

Freddy doesn't say anything, only takes a few steps forward, still snarling. The way he is looking at you, it's like you are something to be stomped on, snapped in half, or swallowed in one bite.

"Freddy?" you squeak. "Freddy, is something wrong?"

He doesn't answer, and you don't need him to. The only thing you are sure of right now is that something is very, *very* wrong with Freddy.

You take an involuntary step back. The moment you do, Freddy charges, mouth open and teeth bared, reaching for you. His paws wrap around your upper arms, hard enough to hurt.

You clamp your eyes shut, letting out a scream as he lifts you from your feet.

Just as quickly, Freddy drops you. Laughter rings out as you land on the hard tile floor, right on your butt.

You open your eyes. Freddy is still above you, but instead of snarling, he's laughing in tandem with Gregory, who has been hidden inside his chest cavity this whole time.

You don't understand. "What . . . what's going on?"

Gregory jumps out of Freddy, still grinning. "Got you! You should have seen the look on your face! You were *so* scared!"

"Oh." It was all a joke. One of Gregory's pranks. You force a smile onto your face. "Yep, you got me," you say, trying to ignore your still-pounding heart. "Nice one."

But no matter how you try to join in, secretly you know that you're not as amused by tonight's antics as Freddy and Gregory are.

➤ **TURN TO PAGE 48.**

Closer inspection of the reception area comes up with fewer options than you'd anticipated. The reception area is mostly open, with a few tables and chairs, and some fake plants, none of which are large enough for you to hide behind. Frustration begins to set in as you search, finally settling on a good, but not great, option: You can hide behind one of the counters. It's not the best cover, though, and even though there's no time to waste, you consider changing tack and heading down into the raceway after all. Then again, if Freddy suspects you're in the raceway, he'd probably be more likely to think you're hiding on the track than in the reception area.

You look behind you, afraid of spotting Freddy on the hunt, as you consider your options. But you need to decide soon. There's no way you're going to be the first one that Freddy finds. Gregory will never let you hear the end of it if he wins the game!

As the seconds tick away, it's almost like you can hear them. There's no more time to waste. With every minute that passes, Freddy might be getting closer!

- **IF YOU WANT TO HIDE BEHIND THE COUNTER IN THE RECEPTION AREA ANYWAY, TURN TO PAGE 29.**
- **IF YOU WANT TO HEAD INTO THE RACEWAY TO HIDE IN ONE OF THE GO-KARTS, TURN TO PAGE 27.**
- **IF YOU WANT TO HIDE IN ONE OF THE RACEWAY GARAGES, TURN TO PAGE 28.**

You rush down the stairs to the raceway. There's not a second to waste. You're careful, though; all the people may be gone from the Pizzaplex but there are still cleaning and security bots around. You look around the course, quickly finding exactly what you're looking for: a demo go-kart set off to the side of the track. It looks a little small to be a hiding place, but when you reach it, you breathe a sigh of relief. There's the perfect amount of room for you to get in and hide if you scrunch down and pull yourself into a ball. Best of all, once you do that, you'll be totally invisible, and there's no way Freddy will think to look for you in such a tight space!

You climb into the car, arranging yourself until you fit in a comfortable way. (Well, mostly comfortable.) Then, you wait.

As time ticks by, your perfect hide-and-seek spot grows less and less comfortable. Still, it's such a good place to hide that you do your best to adjust to the discomfort, shifting your arms and legs as best you can when they start to ache. You're in the middle of one of these rearrangements when you hear a noise coming from somewhere out in the raceway. You freeze. Whatever it is, it's faint, but it kind of sounds like . . . footsteps?

It could be nothing. Or it could be Freddy, or even Gregory. On one hand, you could remain hidden and hope whoever—or whatever—it is passes by without getting close. But what if it *is* Freddy? If he's getting close, but not too close, you might have a chance to slip away to another hiding spot before he discovers where you are.

You clench your toes (your leg is starting to fall asleep), and ponder what to do.

➤ **IF YOU WANT TO REMAIN HIDDEN, TURN TO PAGE 30.**

➤ **IF YOU WANT TO PEEK OUT AND SEE WHAT'S MOVING AROUND, TURN TO PAGE 31.**

You head down into the raceway. When you're not in a rush, you like to admire the grand, twisting track and remember how many times you've driven the go-karts over it. Sometimes, when you don't feel like racing, you love simply sitting in the spectator stands, cheering on the races that run from the moment the Pizzaplex opens until it closes at night. But right now, you have a mission, and you can't get distracted. (Though you may ask Gregory if you can race go-karts once your game of hide-and-seek is over.)

On one side of the raceway, garages run along the wall, fitted with workbenches and all the tools needed to maintain the go-karts in their top condition. You spot one garage that has a bunch of gray storage crates stacked in one corner, piled up nearly to the ceiling. A perfect place to hide!

You head into the garage and work your way into the space behind the crates, which is just large enough to give you a nice space to sit and wait. Which you do. It's a good hiding spot, though there's one problem: You can't see the raceway from your vantage point. Also, the crates muffle what little noise there is. With nothing to see and unable to hear if anyone is getting close, it doesn't take long for you to grow bored. Gregory's hide-and-seek game seemed like a good idea at first, but waiting to be found isn't quite as exciting as you thought it would be.

But if you don't remain still and quiet, Freddy might hear you. And there's no way you're going to let Gregory win without a fight!

Still, as the minutes pass, you consider ways to break up the boredom. You could peek out around the edge of the crates and keep watch on the raceway. Or . . . some of the crates look like they would open. You could look through them. Who knows what might be inside them?

- **IF YOU WANT TO STAY QUIET AND STILL, TURN TO PAGE 39.**
- **IF YOU WANT TO PEEK OUT AND SEE IF THERE'S ANYTHING HAPPENING ON THE RACEWAY, TURN TO PAGE 40.**
- **IF YOU WANT TO RUMMAGE THROUGH THE CRATES, TURN TO PAGE 41.**

You slip behind the reception desk, only to realize immediately that there's not enough cover, only a narrow counter overhang with an overturned trash can behind it. You quickly figure out that this isn't going to work at all. You need to go back out into the raceway and find a better spot to hide from Freddy. But as you go to do so, something in the pile of scattered garbage catches your eye. You pick away the empty wrappers and discarded soda cans to uncover a key chain. Strangely, it's a Bonnie key chain you've never seen before. You thought you'd seen most of the prizes and souvenirs that the Pizzaplex had to offer, but this one is new to you—even though it looks old and well-used. Still, it's cool, so you grab it and put it in your bag.

Unfortunately, it's not going to help you find a place to hide. That's still on you!

➤ ADD BONNIE KEY CHAIN TO YOUR INVENTORY AND RETURN TO PAGE 8.

You decide it seems wiser to remain hidden. You're not going to lose to Gregory just because Freddy manages to spot you peeking out from within the go-kart. Even if it *is* getting more uncomfortable with every passing minute.

The noises grow louder. Then: "Caaaassssiiiieee . . . Grrreeeegggooorryyy . . . where are you?"

It's Freddy for sure. Good thing you weren't tempted to accidentally reveal yourself! You grin. Freddy is moving through the raceway, obviously searching for you, but it doesn't sound like he's headed in your—

Crash!

You jolt at the loud noise coming from nearby.

"Cassie! Gregory!" This time, Freddy yells your names. And unlike earlier, it doesn't sound like he's having fun. He almost sounds . . . angry.

Your heart starts to pound as more loud crashing sounds ensue as if things are being thrown about. You also hear increasingly loud growls from Freddy. You're too afraid to look, but from what you can make out, it sounds like he's becoming more and more agitated.

This was supposed to be a game!

Something must be wrong with Freddy—you're not going to show yourself now. You can wait until Freddy moves on, then go find Gregory. Freddy listens to him more than he listens to you. Gregory will know what to do.

Increasingly nervous, you scrunch down even more, but as you do, a spasm grips your nearly asleep leg. You accidentally kick out, your foot banging against the side of the go-kart.

Oh no.

➤ **TURN TO PAGE 33.**

Curiosity about the noises on the raceway gets the better of you. Shifting as slowly as you can, you untwist yourself from the confines of the go-kart until you are in a position to take a discreet look outside it. At first, all you see is the raceway—drenched in purple neon light, with the huge visages of Roxy looking down upon it. Could what you're hearing be Roxy? You hope so. She'd know the raceway better than Freddy would. Maybe you can ask her if there are any better places to use as a hiding spot.

But you seem to be alone. For a moment, all you can hear is the rise and fall of your own breath. Then, finally, a long shadow slides into view. You inhale and hold your breath, thinking it's Freddy, but then a security bot wheels into your line of sight.

You exhale. Just a stupid bot on its rounds, keeping an "eye" on the Pizzaplex after-hours. You're used to them; you see them every night. Half the time they don't seem to notice you, even when you sneak by them so close that you could touch them. Except . . .

You look at the bot again. This time, it's looking directly at you.

Another moment passes. And then the bot begins to make a bunch of noise. You duck back into the go-kart, but it's too late. The ruckus is definitely drawing attention. Barely a minute passes before you hear Freddy approaching.

"Cassie? Gregory? Is that you?" He sounds . . . strange. "I know you're here." He growls in a way you've never heard before. "And I'm going to find you!"

There's a sudden crunching sound and the noises the security bot was making cut off abruptly. A crash follows as if something is overturned.

"YOU CAN'T HIDE FROM ME FOREVER."

You scrunch your body tighter, a bad feeling growing in your stomach. What is wrong with Freddy? Why is he acting so strangely?

Part of you wants to run, to go find Gregory. The other part of you is confused. Maybe you should reveal yourself, talk to Freddy? He's probably just taking the game way too seriously!

- **IF YOU WANT TO TRY TO RUN AWAY TO FIND GREGORY, TURN TO PAGE 35.**
- **IF YOU WANT TO TRY TALKING TO FREDDY, TURN TO PAGE 37.**

Your heart jumps into your throat as you freeze, trying to ignore the tingling sensation in your leg. Holding your breath, you wait. For a moment, it seems like nothing is going to happen. Is Freddy still out in the raceway? Or has he gotten far enough away that he didn't hear you kick the side of the car?

"I FOUND YOU!"

The roar is accompanied by the heavy tread of footsteps sprinting toward you. Alarmed, you try to free yourself from the go-kart, but it's hard to move quickly and your leg is fully asleep, which isn't helping!

It's too late. Freddy appears above you, a wild look on his face, turning your blood cold. His animatronic eyes narrow.

"I found you, Cassie," he says quieter this time, but in a way that makes your stomach twist. "You *lose*."

Your mouth drops open—to talk to Freddy, to plea—but nothing comes out. Not until he grabs you, hands clamping down on your shoulders, and pulls you from the go-kart.

When that happens, you scream.

His grip tightens and your eyes fill with tears. Then, suddenly, he lets you go. You drop to the floor with a thud. As you blink to clear your vision, Freddy takes a step back. His chest pops open. Inside is Gregory, laughing hysterically.

"I got you!" As he climbs out of Freddy, the animatronic bear starts chuckling along with him. "Wow, Cassie, you were really scared!"

A prank. That's all it was: another one of Gregory's jokes.

They continue laughing, but to you, it wasn't very funny. Still, you smile along with them, wiping the tears from your cheeks. "Oh. Yeah. I guess you fooled me." You get to your feet, shaking your sleeping leg back awake.

"You should have seen your face when Freddy grabbed you," Gregory continues, grinning ear to ear. "Like you thought he was going to eat you or something."

"I would never really hurt you," Freddy adds. And he seems to believe it.

If only you could, too.

➤ **TURN TO PAGE 48.**

The next crash sounds a little farther off, and you make a decision: to try to find Gregory. You're careful to climb out of the go-kart quietly, so as not to give yourself away. Where the security bot had stood moments ago is now a pile of what can only be described as metal shards and fragments. Freddy isn't anywhere around here. Is he still in Roxy Raceway? You can't see everywhere, so you're not sure, but if you're quick, it's a straight shot to the stairs. If you can run up them, it's a relatively easy way back into the Pizzaplex.

Still looking at the dismantled pile of security bot, fear grips you, and you begin to run. You bolt across the raceway. You make it most of the way across, and the stairs appear to be within reach when a huge shadow emerges at the edge of your vision. Two hands reach out and grab you, then twist you around.

It's Freddy. At least, you think it is. There's a wild look in his eyes. It's Freddy, but not the same fun Freddy you started the game with.

"F-F-Freddy . . ." you stammer. "What are you doing?" You ask the question, but something tells you that you're not going to get an answer.

At least, not one you like.

"I found you," he growls. "And that means you lose." Freddy's grip tightens painfully. "Time to pay the price."

After that, all you can see is teeth.

You can't help it—you scream.

A moment later, Freddy's grip suddenly loosens, releasing you. Freddy's chest bursts open, revealing Gregory, who is laughing hysterically. He jumps down, barely able to catch his breath.

"You should have seen how scared you were!" he manages between giggles. "I got you!"

You blush, realizing that this was all a joke. One of Gregory's pranks. Except . . . you really were scared.

"I told you the game would be fun!" Gregory says.

You smile weakly, mostly so he doesn't feel like you are being a sore loser. "Yeah," you say, forcing a smile onto your face. "Fun."

But quietly, you hope for a different game, and a different kind of fun, tomorrow.

➤ **TURN TO PAGE 48.**

Whatever Freddy is doing, he's clearly taking this game of hide-and-seek too far. You wish Gregory were here—Freddy listens to him better than he listens to you—but he's not. Which means that you have to deal with the animatronic.

You climb out of the car. "Freddy! Hey!"

Freddy has started to move away, leaving behind the remains of the security bot—now a crumpled pile of pieces—but he freezes as he hears your voice. Slowly, he turns.

You do not like the look in his eyes.

"What are you doing, Cassie?" Freddy says slowly, in a low voice. "You are supposed to hide from me."

"I know." You take a careful step closer, holding up your hands. "But I think you are taking this game too seriously, Freddy. It's supposed to be fun."

Freddy's eyes narrow. "But I *am* having fun."

"Well, you found me, which means Gregory wins. Let's go find him. We can look together—"

"But I don't need to find Gregory," Freddy cuts in, a little louder. He starts moving menacingly toward you. "I found you. Which means you lose."

You step back again, but the car is still behind you. There's nowhere to go. "Freddy—"

"YOU LOSE, CASSIE!"

Freddy lunges at you. You scream in terror.

Then, an instant before he reaches you, Freddy stops. His chest opens up, revealing Gregory within. He's laughing.

"You lose, Cassie!" he says in a mocking voice.

Freddy joins him, chuckling, and looking way more normal than a moment ago.

And that's when you get it. There was nothing wrong with Freddy. It was all a prank orchestrated by Gregory to scare you. You relax, though your heart is still pounding in your chest.

"Ha ha," you say, "yeah, I guess you fooled me."

"You should have seen how scared you were!" Gregory jumps out of Freddy and to the floor, nearly doubling over with laughter. "Told you this game would be fun."

You smile and say nothing.

Sometimes you think that you and Gregory have very different ideas of fun.

➤ TURN TO PAGE 48.

You decide the best course of action is to remain quiet. Which turns out to be a good idea, because just a few minutes later you hear your name being called.

"Caaasssiieeeee . . ." It's Freddy! He's in the raceway somewhere, but you can't tell where without peeking out and risking revealing yourself. "Grrreeeggggooorryy . . . where aaarrre youuuuu?"

You smile to yourself. This hiding place is too good. There's no way Freddy is going to find you here. All you need to do is stay quiet until he passes through the raceway.

CRASH!

"Ready or not, I'm going to find you!"

The anger in Freddy's voice causes you to flinch. Almost as much as the crashing noise does, which is quickly followed by another one. It sounds like Freddy is overturning tables and chairs, but you're too afraid to look out. It sounds like something is wrong with Freddy.

"YOU CAN'T HIDE FOREVER!"

Very wrong.

You swallow, unsure of what to do. As soon as Freddy leaves the raceway, you can try to find Gregory. Freddy listens to him more than he listens to you. Gregory will know what to do.

BANG!

This time, the crashing sound is closer. *Much* closer. The crates shift and rattle, and you realize in horror that Freddy is just on the other side of the pile, pulling the crates away. If you don't do something quick, he's going to find you. Your heart starts to pound, mouth going dry. You can try to run. Or even hide in one of the nearest crates.

On the other side of the pile, another crate is pulled away.

"I'm going to find you . . ." Freddy growls, sounding more menacing than you've ever heard him be before.

Whatever you do, you need to do it fast!

➤ **IF YOU WANT TO TRY TO RUN, TURN TO PAGE 42.**

➤ **IF YOU WANT TO HIDE IN A CRATE, TURN TO PAGE 43.**

Unable to contain your curiosity and suppress your boredom, you sneak over to the edge of the crates and peek around. The moment you do, Freddy stomps into view. Abruptly, he stops. You freeze as his head slowly swivels your way.

He's spotted you.

A smile starts to form on your lips—you lost, but oh well, it was only a game—when Freddy's face crumples into a frown. He bares his teeth at you, and his eyes take on a manic glow.

"I found you, Cassie." The words rumble out of him, a low growl. "You lose."

Suddenly, he rushes at you. There's no time to figure out what's wrong with him, or why; you barely manage to duck back behind the pile of crates before Freddy is tearing through them, tossing them aside like they are made of cardboard.

"Youloseyouloseyouloseyoulose," he rants.

Your stomach clenches. This was supposed to be a fun game. So why is Freddy acting like this?

You press up against the wall. Gregory would know what's happening, know what to do. Maybe if you run, you can slip past Freddy and find him. Or maybe Freddy is simply taking this too seriously. If you plead with him, maybe he'll calm down, and you two can go and find Gregory together.

The crates rattle and crash as he continues to dismantle the pile.

Whatever you do, you need to do it fast!

➤ **IF YOU WANT TO TRY TO RUN AND FIND GREGORY, TURN TO PAGE 45.**

➤ **IF YOU WANT TO PLEAD WITH FREDDY, TURN TO PAGE 46.**

You decide to pass the time by checking out the crates. After all, what harm could it do?

There are a few crates nearby that don't seemed to be locked. You open the first but are disappointed. It's completely empty. The second crate is almost as bad; there are only a few scraps of packing material in the bottom. Sure, you weren't expecting to find treasure, but certainly something a little more interesting than that!

Finally, you open the last crate. It, too, is mostly empty, except for one item, tucked into a corner. It's a glass jar. You pick it up. The jar is filled with a whole bunch of metal screws and bolts, of all sizes. Not exactly exciting, but you decide to take it anyway. After all, you never know what might be useful later!

Not much to do now but wait . . . Or is there?

- **ADD JAR OF SCREWS AND BOLTS TO YOUR INVENTORY. IF YOU WANT TO STAY QUIET AND STILL, TURN TO PAGE 39.**
- **ADD JAR OF SCREWS AND BOLTS TO YOUR INVENTORY. IF YOU WANT TO PEEK OUT AND SEE IF THERE'S ANYTHING HAPPENING ON THE RACEWAY, TURN TO PAGE 40.**

Freddy continues to rip the crates away, one by one, inching closer. You can't wait any longer. You need to find Gregory, which means you need to *run*.

You make a break for it, slipping through the narrow opening between the crates and the wall. Occupied with the pile, Freddy doesn't seem to notice you at first, giving you the chance to get out of the garage and back onto the floor of the raceway. The stairs up to the entrance aren't far, you just need to—

A hand clamps down on your shoulder and yanks you backward.

"Found you!" Freddy roars in your ears.

"Freddy, what are you doing?" You try to struggle, but you can barely breathe as he pulls you into a bear hug, his arms wrapping around you and getting tighter . . . tighter . . .

"I found you," Freddy growls into your ear. "That means *you lose*."

The hug draws even tighter. You fight, but it doesn't do any good. Freddy is far too strong.

The last of your breath comes out as a scream.

Then, suddenly, you drop to the floor. You gasp, able to breathe again, and twist around, ready to run. But as you watch, Freddy's chest bursts open, revealing Gregory inside. He's laughing.

"Wh-what?" you stammer. "Gregory, what are you—?"

"Got you!" he announces, and suddenly, you understand. It was a joke. A *prank*. "You were so scared, I thought you were going to pee your pants!"

Freddy begins to chuckle along with him as Gregory climbs down from his chest cavity.

"Heh . . ." You try to join in, but you are definitely not feeling as amused as they are. Your heart is still pounding, and your shoulder hurts where Freddy grabbed it. "Yeah, I guess you got me."

"See?" says Gregory. "I told you this would be a fun game!"

You smile to appease him but secretly hope for a different kind of fun tomorrow night.

➤ **TURN TO PAGE 48.**

Freddy is getting closer. There's no way you'll be able to run without him spotting you, so you decide to try hiding inside a crate instead and hope he doesn't think to look inside. You go to the closest one, pull the top open, and climb in. Then, you shut it, plunging yourself into pure darkness. Now, all you can hear is the banging and thudding of Freddy working his way through the crates, and the thick pounding of your heart in your ears. You hold your breath, hoping that when Freddy doesn't find you, he moves on to search somewhere else.

"Where are youuuuuu?" Freddy's voice is muffled by the walls of the crate, but the sound of it still makes your stomach tighten. Why is he acting so strange?

Your heart drums louder and louder. And then, suddenly, you realize that's all you can hear. No more crates crashing around. No more Freddy calling your name.

Has he given up? Moved on?

You count down, resolving to take a peek outside if you don't hear anything after a minute.

Fifty-nine . . . fifty-eight . . .

It's getting harder to breathe. But it must be in your head. You haven't been in the crate long enough for all the air to be gone.

Twenty-five . . . twenty-four . . .

The silence persists. Freddy must have left, you tell yourself, gone to look for you or Gregory somewhere else.

Three . . . two . . .

Suddenly, the top of the crate flies open, revealing Freddy standing above you. His eyes are wild, his teeth bared.

"I found you, Cassie." He growls in a way that chills your blood. "You lose."

As he reaches for you, you clamp your eyes shut and scream.

But instead of feeling Freddy's claws close around you, the sound of laughter rings out. When you open your eyes again, Freddy's chest is open, and Gregory is peeking out.

"Fooled you!" Gregory cries, and continues laughing.

"This was . . . a *joke*?" You sit up, confused.

"Yup," Gregory says, and grins. "I got you good! You should have seen your face when Freddy reached for you!"

He continues laughing, and you chuckle along with him, so he doesn't think you're a bad sport. But, secretly, you don't think the prank was as funny as Gregory does.

➤ **TURN TO PAGE 48.**

Freddy has already seen you, so you might as well make a run for it. You slip through the opening behind the crates, then around the go-kart being repaired in the garage, putting it between you and Freddy. But he spots you immediately, tossing away one last crate before coming straight for you. One clawed hand reaches for the go-kart, tossing it aside like it's a toy car.

You can't help it. You freeze, backed up against the workbench as Freddy approaches. You open your mouth, but it's like your voice is broken, and you can only manage a squeak as Freddy reaches for you with both hands and clamps down on your arms. He shakes you, which finally dislodges the scream from your throat. You want to fight, but Freddy is too strong.

There's nothing you can do except close your eyes and hope it's over fast.

Then, suddenly, Freddy stops shaking you. A moment later, you drop to the floor of the garage, landing hard on the concrete. Familiar laughter rings out. When you look up again, blinking away the tears, Freddy's chest is wide-open. Gregory hops out of it, nearly doubled over in amusement as he points at you.

"We fooled you, Cassie!" says Freddy jovially. He looks and sounds normal again.

"We did!" cries Gregory. "You should have seen the look on your face!"

Slowly, you understand. Gregory's game for tonight wasn't a game. It was a joke, another one of his pranks.

You try to laugh along with them. "Hah, yeah. I guess you got me."

"See?" says Gregory. "I told you tonight would be awesome!"

You nod, even though you wish you'd played a real game of hide-and-seek. But you don't want Gregory to think you're a bad sport, so you keep that to yourself and quietly hope that tomorrow night is fun for the *both* of you.

➤ TURN TO PAGE 48.

Freddy is getting closer, the pile of crates getting smaller and smaller.

"Freddy!" you cry out. "What are you doing? Why are you acting like this?"

"I found you," he cries, refusing to stop. "You lose, Cassie!"

You gasp for breath, terrified as Freddy continues to dig his way to you. *Where is Gregory?* you wonder. *What would he do in this situation?*

"You found me!" you finally sob. It's the only thing you can think to do. "I give up!"

At last, Freddy breaks through the crates. Then, he stops and simply stares at you.

You relax. You gave up. That's all you needed to do, apparently.

Suddenly, Freddy's scowl deepens. He bares his teeth and repeats, "You lose, Cassie." You've never heard him sound like this before, in a way that makes your blood run cold. Whatever is coming next, you know it's going to be bad.

"And now," Freddy says, "you have to pay the price."

He reaches for you. Cornered, the only thing you can do is close your eyes and scream.

Suddenly, the sound of laughter fills your ears.

When you open your eyes again, Freddy has taken a step back. His chest is open. Inside sits Gregory, grinning ear to ear.

"Ha!" He climbs out of Freddy's chest, dropping to the floor. "We got you!"

"Yes, Cassie," Freddy says happily, sounding like his normal self again. "We got you."

Your cheeks turn warm as you understand. This was one of Gregory's pranks. He didn't want to play a game of hide-and-seek—he was trying to scare you. "Oh," you say, tongue-tied. "Yes, you fooled me."

"You were really scared there for a second," says Gregory. "Don't worry, Cassie. It was just a fun game, like I said it would be!"

You smile reluctantly. "Yeah, it was," you say.
Even though, deep inside, you don't totally agree.

➤ **TURN TO PAGE 48.**

NIGHT 2

The entrance doors to the Pizzaplex snap shut, locking after the last patrons leave. Once again, you and Gregory emerge from your hiding place, ready for another night of hijinks. Gregory seems in high spirits, but after what happened last night, you're feeling nervous and a little reluctant as he leads you back to the Glamrock Band's greenrooms.

"Don't worry," Gregory reassures you as you head up the lobby stairs. "No tricks tonight. We can play a *real* game of hide-and-seek."

You slow down a little as you get close to Freddy's greenroom. "I don't know. Why don't we play hide-and-seek alone tonight? Just the two of us. Whoever hides from the other the longest wins the game."

Gregory scoffs. "What fun is that? Besides"—he passes by Freddy's room without going in—"I've already set tonight's game up."

He turns into Monty's greenroom and heads over to the animatronic, who is leaning against the wall. The Glamrock gator appears to be waiting for the two of you.

You hesitate in the doorway. "What do you mean?"

Gregory grins. "Freddy is taking the night off. Tonight, I programmed Monty to play with us. We'll hide, and he'll seek."

You look at Monty, who grins. "I'm ready to rock and roll, Gregory. Let's do this!" He gives you two scaly thumbs-up.

You consider the proposition. It *would* be fun to play a real game of hide-and-seek in the Pizzaplex, but it's hard to forget last night. "No tricks?"

"No tricks," Gregory promises.

"Okay," you agree.

"Great! Give us a head start," he says to Monty. Then, to you: "C'mon." He grabs your arm and pulls you back into the hallway.

"Where should we hide?" you say. "How about Monty's Gator

Golf? Maybe he won't think to look in his own part of the Pizzaplex."

Gregory rolls his eyes. "No way. I have a much better idea: We should go hide in Bonnie Bowl!" Without waiting for you, he dashes off, leaving you unsure whether to follow or hide on your own.

"Wait!" you call after him. "What if we hide together someplace Monty never goes, like the backstage office—where the stage controls are?"

- IF YOU WANT TO FOLLOW GREGORY AND HIDE IN BONNIE BOWL, TURN TO PAGE 50.
- IF YOU WANT TO HIDE ALONE IN MONTY'S GATOR GOLF, TURN TO PAGE 51.
- IF YOU WANT TO COMPROMISE AND HIDE IN THE BACKSTAGE OFFICE, TURN TO PAGE 52.

Gregory doesn't wait for you. After thinking for a moment, you rush after him, toward Bonnie Bowl. It's not your first choice for a hiding place, but it's where Gregory wants to go, and if you stick close to him, it's unlikely that he can pull off any more pranks like last night.

You try to catch up, but there's a pair of security bots in the Pizzaplex lobby, which you have to avoid. It delays you, and you make it to Bonnie Bowl just in time to see Gregory at the opposite end of the entrance atrium, heading into the bowling area. You go that way, too. As much as Roxy Raceway is your favorite part of the Pizzaplex, you do like Bonnie Bowl. It has a cool vintage look, and it also is home to the best ice cream.

"Gregory!" you call after him as loudly as you dare, afraid to draw attention from the bots, or worse, Monty. "Wait up!"

Either he doesn't hear you or he doesn't care because he goes directly for a door down near the far end of the lanes. You think it leads to the area behind the bowling lanes, where the pins get reset. It's a good place to hide, and you're a little bummed that Gregory thought of it before you did. He opens the door and goes in, letting the door shut behind him. Once you reach it, you try to follow, but it's locked, and you don't know the code for the keypad beside it. You pound on the door.

"Gregory! Let me in!" You wait, then try pounding on the door again, but he doesn't reply.

Your head start must be running out soon. Giving up on Gregory, you look around. The ice-cream parlor jumps out at you first. What better place to hide than somewhere with delicious frozen treats? But as you scan the bowling lanes, your eyes are drawn to Bonnie's old stage, surrounded by a heavy velvet curtain. Bonnie hasn't performed in ages, but maybe his stage would make a good hiding spot?

➤ **IF YOU WANT TO HIDE IN THE ICE-CREAM PARLOR, TURN TO PAGE 54.**

➤ **IF YOU WANT TO CHECK OUT BONNIE'S OLD STAGE, TURN TO PAGE 55.**

You bet Monty's Gator Golf is a much better place to hide than the bowling area or the backstage office area, and you'll prove it by winning the game of hide-and-seek!

You pass by the greenrooms. Again, Roxy isn't around, and your heart sinks a little. You miss her! Maybe once your game of hide-and-seek is over, Gregory will help you find her. But that's a plan for later. Right now, you need to focus on finding the best place to hide in Gator Golf.

And proving that Gregory isn't always as clever as he thinks he is.

You make your way to the golf course and through the lobby, passing beneath its weird decorations on the ceiling. On one hand, you like Gator Golf's tropical theme, with all its fake palm trees and vines draped everywhere. On the other hand, the fake rivers with their real water always makes this area smell a little . . . well, swampy. But it's dark and twisty, and enough like a bayou that you know there are plenty of great places to hide.

You pause just inside, debating whether to head down to the actual golf course or check out the snack bar to see if there are any good spots there. The golf course is bigger, with more nooks and crannies, but the snack bar might have *snacks*. And that sounds pretty great if you're going to be hiding from Monty for a while.

➤ **IF YOU WANT TO HIDE ON THE MINI GOLF COURSE, TURN TO PAGE 67.**

➤ **IF YOU WANT TO FIND A PLACE TO HIDE IN THE SNACK BAR, TURN TO PAGE 69.**

Upon hearing your suggestion, Gregory slows, thinking for a moment. Which is a bit of a surprise. He has a tendency to ignore your suggestions.

"Hm," he says. "The backstage office might actually be a good place to hide? Maybe Monty won't think to look somewhere so close to the greenrooms."

You suppress a smile as he comes back. It's nice to be listened to for once!

It's a short trip to the backstage office, but the moment you get inside, your mood sinks. There's no obvious place where two kids can hide. Maybe you could get under the consoles that run along the wall, but if Monty thinks to check in here, he'll spot you right away. And there's nothing else to hide behind or in. You blush, wishing your suggestion had been better.

Gregory scowls as he looks around. "No way this is gonna work!"

He doesn't bother to search any closer, or discuss it further with you, as he only turns around and leaves. You hesitate, torn between taking the time to look around more or finding a more promising place to hide from Monty. And now Gregory isn't even around to help you decide.

➤ IF YOU WANT TO GO BACK AND HIDE IN MONTY'S GATOR GOLF, TURN TO PAGE 51.

➤ IF YOU WANT TO SEARCH THE BACKSTAGE OFFICE FURTHER, TURN TO PAGE 53.

You haven't given up on hiding in the backstage office quite yet. You do a sweep of the room, looking over all the control panels. With their buttons and lights and switches, they are as tempting as candy, and you wish the game hadn't started so you could play with them instead. Gregory isn't the only one who loves programming and techy stuff. But you aren't sure how long a head start Monty is going to give you, so there's no time to waste.

Hiding under the consoles isn't going to work. You find a few promising panel doors set into the wall, probably for storage, but unfortunately, they are all locked. As time ticks by, it becomes increasingly clear that this idea is a bust.

You are about to head somewhere else to hide when a shiny glimmer of red catches your eye. On top of the filing cabinet, someone has stashed a can of Sodaroni. The night is long, and you might get thirsty while you hide, so you take it. At least you got one thing out of your visit to the backstage office! You figure you might as well head to Monty's Gator Golf . . .

➤ **ADD A CAN OF SODARONI TO YOUR INVENTORY AND TURN TO PAGE 51.**

Ice cream it is. Let Gregory have his hiding place behind the lanes. You will be in the ice-cream parlor, enjoying a frosty cone while you hide from Monty. You head over to the concession area, which looks like an old-timey soda fountain, all chrome finish with black-and-white checkered tile. A deactivated worker drone is slumped over the counter, but that's okay. You're happy to serve yourself.

But before you indulge in a sweet treat, you look for a good spot to hide. Unfortunately, most of the counter has glass windows in the front, leaving only a curved area as a possibility. You're about to head to the back area of the parlor when you hear something in the distance.

"Oh yeaahhhh!" It's Monty! "Here I come!"

No time to look further. Or indulge your sweet tooth.

"You can't hide from me! I'm gonna find you kids!"

Are you imagining it, or does Monty sound . . . angrier than usual? There's more of a growl in his voice than there was in the greenroom.

At least, you think so? You're not sure, but if you don't hide quickly, Monty is going to find you standing out in the open like you're trying to lose the game! You could jump behind the counter, but what if Monty decides to snoop back there? The only other quick option you see is a trash can. You hesitate, wasting precious seconds as you debate which option would be best.

➤ **IF YOU WANT TO HIDE IN THE TRASH CAN, TURN TO PAGE 57.**

➤ **IF YOU HIDE BEHIND THE COUNTER, TURN TO PAGE 59.**

You're curious enough about Bonnie's old stage that you wander over to it. It's surrounded by a velvet curtain, with a sign that says the attraction is temporarily closed, which has been there as long as you can remember. Dust tickles your nose as you pull aside the curtain, letting what little light there is from the neon signs fall inside.

The small stage is empty, save for more dust and a few stray, discarded napkins. But a door on the back wall draws your attention. Even from here, you can tell that it's locked, with no indication of where it goes. *Strange*, you think.

But there's no time to ponder it. There are noises behind you, coming from back toward the entrance to Bonnie Bowl.

"Oh yeaahhhh," Monty croons in his rough rock and roll voice. "Here I come!"

Shoot. You weren't paying attention, and now you're almost out of time to find a hiding spot. Your options are limited with Monty nearly upon you. You could hide behind the curtain—maybe Monty wouldn't think to check an area that's been out of commission for so long—or . . .

The only other option you see is a nearby trash can. If you're quick, you should have just enough time to get the top off and climb in.

➤ IF YOU WANT TO HIDE BEHIND THE STAGE CURTAIN, TURN TO PAGE 56.

➤ IF YOU WANT TO HIDE IN THE TRASH CAN, TURN TO PAGE 57.

With no time to lose, you climb up on the stage and draw the curtain closed, leaving only a tiny slit through which you can peer out into Bonnie Bowl. You wait, dust tickling your nose, and it's not long before Monty comes stomping into view. Something seems strange about his movements, though. They're twitchier than normal as if he's receiving little jolts of electricity every so often. *Strange*, you think, *but maybe he's due for maintenance?*

"You can't run, you can't hide," Monty half sings, half growls.

Does he *sound* weird, too?

Monty takes a few more steps, head swinging left and right as he surveys Bonnie Bowl, searching. Then, a violent twitch nearly sends him toppling to one side. He catches a table at the last moment, claws scraping over it, leaving deep furrows. Then, suddenly, a cleaning bot comes into view. Normally, Monty would ignore it. But instead, he growls viciously and lunges for it.

"Found you!" His claws sink into the bot. When he rips his hands away, parts of the bot go flying.

Your fingers tighten on the edge of the velvet curtain. That's not right. Is Gregory playing another joke on you? That's what you want to think, but Monty's twitching might indicate something actually wrong. Your mouth goes dry as you realize that if Monty comes closer, he might find you. And if he repeats what he did to that bot . . .

That's only if he looks behind the curtain, you reassure yourself. And maybe he'll leave without bothering to look here. Still, you're scared enough to weigh your other options. The only one that makes any sense is behind you: the door. But it appears to be locked.

➤ **IF YOU REMAIN BEHIND THE CURTAIN AND HOPE MONTY LEAVES, TURN TO PAGE 64.**

➤ **IF YOU HAVE A BONNIE KEY CHAIN, TURN TO PAGE 65.**

You run over to the trash can, praying that the cleaning bots have already emptied it. You're in luck: The bag inside is clean. You climb inside, pulling the top down right as Monty calls out again, this time much closer.

"You kids can run, but you can't hide!"

Through the flap at the top of the trash can, you see Monty lumber into the bowling area. His voice sounds angry, but maybe that is part of Gregory's programming. After all, he promised no tricks tonight.

"I'm gonna fff-ff-fiiiii . . . !" Monty's head suddenly jerks to one side as if an electrical jolt hit him. "Find you!"

A nervous feeling grows in the pit of your stomach. Monty doesn't sound or look right. His body is twitching in a way you've never seen before.

Suddenly, a cleaning drone buzzes by. Drawn to the movement, Monty whips around, his tail colliding with the bot, which goes flying. The moment it lands, Monty descends upon it, claws flashing as he rips the bot apart.

The sickening feeling grows. You let the flap of the trash can fall shut. Is this another one of Gregory's jokes? After all, Monty is acting a little like Freddy did last night. But Gregory isn't hiding in Monty, and you saw him go through the door. Plus there's that weird twitching . . .

The growls and tearing sounds grow louder. Then, slowly, they fade away, leaving you in a dark silence. You wait, heart pounding in your chest. It has to be another joke. That's why Gregory dashed off and left you. Better safe than sorry, though. You wait until it's been silent for a while, then slowly lift the top of the trash can off. Bonnie Bowl is empty, save for what remains of the cleaning bot.

There's a low growl behind you.

You turn, coming face-to-face with Monty. Toothy snout opening, he raises his claws.

You have just enough time to understand that this isn't a joke before Monty grabs you.

GAME OVER

➤ TO START FROM THE BEGINNING, TURN TO PAGE 3.
➤ TO TRY THIS NIGHT AGAIN, TURN TO PAGE 48.

You leap onto the counter and slide over it, then crouch beneath the overhang. It's dark back here, but you feel something against your foot as you shift into a comfortable position. Reaching out, you pick up a metal, cylindrical object. It's an ice-cream scoop. *Perfect*, you think. Once you elude Monty and he moves on, you can make yourself a sundae.

You put the ice-cream scoop in your bag as, back in the bowling lanes, you hear more noise. The heavy, stomping footsteps give away the source: Monty, getting closer.

"I know you're here!" This is followed by a low growl. Monty always sounds a little grizzled—he's a rock and roll alligator, after all—but there's an edge to his words that you don't like. He doesn't sound like he did earlier.

There's a new sound now, too: a cleaning bot. You can't see it from where you're hiding, but you're pretty sure that's what it is. Monty should ignore it. And hopefully it won't come around the counter and give you away.

"I FOUND YOU!"

You jump and nearly scream, expecting to look up and see Monty standing above you, only to realize he doesn't sound close enough. Instead, you hear a crunching sound, followed by the high scream of metal being torn apart. You clamp a hand over your mouth and risk a peek. In the corner of the ice-cream parlor, Monty is bent over a now-twisted pile of what used to be a cleaning bot. You retreat back behind the counter. Monty isn't supposed to do *that*!

Is this another one of Gregory's games? Or has something gone awry with Monty's programming?

Either way, it seems like a good idea to try to escape to somewhere else. Somewhere safer. You could sneak out of the parlor while Monty is still occupied with the bot. Or make a break for it, head for the door Gregory went through, and try to get your friend's attention. Your heart pounds as you consider what to do.

- ADD ICE-CREAM SCOOP TO YOUR INVENTORY. IF YOU WANT TO SNEAK OUT OF THE ICE-CREAM PARLOR, TURN TO PAGE 61.
- ADD ICE-CREAM SCOOP TO YOUR INVENTORY. IF YOU WANT TO MAKE A BREAK FOR THE DOOR IN THE BOWLING LANES, TURN TO PAGE 62.

Quiet and slow seems like the smarter choice to you. If you follow along the counter, staying crouched down, you should be able to sneak out before Monty notices, even with the glass fronts. You'll just have to be *extra* quiet. You take a deep breath and hold it, afraid your pounding heart will give you away. Then, you start to make your way along the counter.

Luckily, Monty is still occupied with tearing apart the bot. You move as fast as you dare, making it halfway, reaching the server bot that's slumped over in its nighttime deactivation mode. It's in the way, but you quietly slip around it, taking care not to accidentally bump it.

"Ice-cream time!" Suddenly, the server bot springs to life. Its eyes light up and it twists toward you, brandishing an ice-cream scoop like a weapon. "Would you like some ice cream?"

"I FOUND YOU!" The server bot's flailing alerts Monty. He drops the cleaning bot and comes racing toward you, teeth bared, claws out.

You run.

Or at least, you try to.

Monty grabs you before you can run out from around the corner. You can't help it—you scream.

"I give up!" But Monty's claws tighten painfully as he lifts you. "Monty, you win! Gregory! Gregory, where are you? This isn't funny!"

Monty's jaws draw closer.

This isn't funny at all.

GAME OVER

➤ TO START FROM THE BEGINNING, TURN TO PAGE 3.
➤ TO TRY THIS NIGHT AGAIN, TURN TO PAGE 48.

You decide Monty is too close to risk sneaking out. You need to make a break for it and run! You risk one more peek over the counter to make sure Monty is still distracted by the bot, then jump up and bolt back toward the bowling lanes. You make it to the end of the counter before Monty notices the sound of your footsteps.

"There you are!" he growls, dropping the bot. "Oh, I'm gonna get you! And then I'm gonna rock you!"

You're out of the ice-cream parlor by the time you hear his heavy tread coming after you. But you keep your focus on one thing: the door near the bowling lanes. Gregory is behind there. Gregory will know what to do. Or he'll tell you Monty's behavior is another one of his jokes, in which case you are definitely going to dump a big bowl of chocolate sauce right on his stupid head!

You reach the door and begin pounding on it. "Gregory! Gregory! Let me in!" Your fists hurt as they connect with the metal door. "There's something wrong with Monty!"

"Oh, is there?"

You twist around. Monty is standing only a few steps away, breathing heavily and twitching in a way you've never seen before. He growls, his shiny alligator fangs a rainbow of colors in the neon lights. "Found you."

You want to believe it's another prank. But something about this feels wrong. *Very wrong.*

You press up against the door. "Gregory!" you yell one more time.

Monty reaches for you.

But before he can grab you, you fall back, the door opening up behind you. You hit the floor as Gregory steps forward, brandishing a device.

"Monty, stop!" he cries.

Immediately, Monty deactivates.

You get back to your feet. "That wasn't funny, Gregory! You promised no more pranks!"

He frowns. "It wasn't a prank."

"I don't believe you!"

"No, I swear!" He taps at his device. "Something went wrong with Monty's programming. I don't know what, but . . . I'll figure it out. Before tomorrow night."

You cross your arms, still shaking, not sure you care.

Or that you believe him.

➤ **TURN TO PAGE 88.**

You don't have much of a choice. Drawing the curtain fully closed, you're plunged into pure darkness. Beyond the curtain, Monty continues to stomp around. You can hear his footsteps, low growls, and the occasional *bang* or *crunch*.

"Let's rock!" Monty calls out, sounding too close for comfort. "Don't you want to rock with me?"

You do *not* want to rock with Monty. If this is another one of Gregory's pranks, it's not funny. And you are going to give him a piece of your mind!

Monty is getting closer. You can hear the gator growling now, right beyond the curtain. You're sure if you drew it back now, he'd be right there, close enough to touch. Seconds tick by, sweat beading on your forehead as you listen.

Inhale. Exhale. Inhale. Exhale.

Any moment, you expect Monty to rip the curtain aside.

Then, you hear footsteps again. Monty is moving away.

Thank goodness! You let out the breath you were holding, then inhale. Dust from the old stage travels up your nose.

You try to stop it, but it happens too fast.

"Ah-choo!"

The sneeze sounds like an explosion in the small space. It's followed by the thudding of steps, and before you get a chance to think, Monty tears the curtain away, exposing you.

He growls, eyes wild, teeth bared. "Found you."

You should give up. Plead. *Something.*

But as Monty reaches for you, all you can do is *scream.*

GAME OVER

> **TO START FROM THE BEGINNING, TURN TO PAGE 3.**

> **TO TRY THIS NIGHT AGAIN, TURN TO PAGE 48.**

If you could get through the door of the stage, maybe you'd be safe. Wait! Suddenly you recall the Bonnie key chain you found earlier. Digging it out of your bag, you pop the Bonnie head off to reveal a key. You go over to the door and try to get the key into the lock. It's not easy in the dark, but finally, you get the key in. It fits perfectly!

The moment you turn it, Monty rips the curtain away. He twitches, eyes glowing with fervent anger. "Found you . . ."

Panicking, your fingers nearly slip from the key, but you manage to turn it as Monty jumps onto the stage. You shove the door open and slip in, slamming it shut just in time. Monty's entire weight slams against it, rattling the frame. But, thankfully, it locked behind you. Monty pounds on the door, making feral sounds that cause your blood to run cold.

"Oh, I'm gonna get you!" Monty cries.

Bang! Bang! Bang!

His fists beat against the door. You swallow hard as the frame strains under each blow. The door looked sturdy, but soon you realize that it isn't going to last long. It's all you can do to shakily get to your feet and look around. Your stomach drops as you do. There's nothing here, just some old tables and chairs, and beat-up cardboard cutouts of Bonnie. No other doors. No windows.

You're trapped.

"Help!" You don't know what else to do. "Gregory, help me! Monty has gone crazy!"

"Monty has gone crazy!" Monty echoes in a mocking way.

A splinter of door falls away. The blows pause as an eye appears in it.

Monty says, "There you are . . . gonna get you . . ."

The attack resumes, and within moments, the door is demolished. You back up against the wall, but there's nowhere to run. Nowhere to go.

With a growl, Monty bursts through the remains of the stage door and lunges at you.

You scream.

Right before his claws reach you, Monty suddenly deactivates, his whole body freezing and going limp.

Gasping for breath, you look behind him. Gregory is there on the stage, a device in hand.

"That wasn't funny!" you cry. "You said no more pranks!"

"It wasn't a prank!" Gregory replies. "I swear, I don't know what happened. Something went wrong with his programming."

Mad, and still terrified, you want to yell more. But the way Monty was twitching . . . maybe there *was* something wrong with him.

"I'll fix it before we play again," Gregory promises.

You nod, but you're not sure you want to play any more of Gregory's games.

➤ TURN TO PAGE 88.

The moment you get to the bottom of the stairs to the mini golf course, you spot the perfect place to hide: the giant alligator mouth! You can go all the way into the back of it, where it's dark. Monty will never think to look for you there!

You make your way over and carefully climb into the mouth. The tongue is weirdly soft, but it's shadowed enough in the back of the mouth that you must be invisible from the outside. You get comfortable next to a pair of fangs and wait. As the minutes tick by, you start to regret not grabbing a snack from the snack bar on your way down. Who knows how long it will take Monty to—

Suddenly, you hear noises in the distance, getting louder. Crouching lower, you watch as Monty comes into view, making his way across the mini golf course. He's moving slowly and deliberately, searching as he goes. You stifle a giggle. He's carrying a golf club as if he plans to play a few holes while he looks.

"Gonna find you," he calls, stomping down the stairs. At the bottom, he seems to jerk, almost missing the last step and stumbling a little. "Find you," he repeats, with another spasm, this time in his arm.

The last few words sound angry, and you start to feel uneasy. Monty continues onto the course, muttering and jerking in a way that doesn't seem right. Or is this another one of Gregory's pranks? You're going to be so mad if he pulls that again.

"I KNOW YOU'RE HERE!" Monty suddenly screeches, then raises the golf club and swings, smashing one of the hole markers.

You throw a hand over your mouth to keep from making a noise as the giant gator moves out of sight. What's wrong with Monty? Another joke . . . it has to be.

But the way Monty is moving, as if there's something wrong with his limbs . . . Freddy didn't act like that. Uneasiness fills you. Maybe you need to get out of here before Monty finds you. Make a distraction and run. Or just keep watching him, see if he gets any weirder. There's also a fearful part of you that's saying to just stay hidden, let Monty move on.

You're not sure what to do.

- IF YOU WANT TO PEEK OUT OF THE GATOR HEAD AND WATCH MONTY, TURN TO PAGE 70.
- IF YOU HAVE A JAR OF SCREWS AND BOLTS AND WANT TO USE IT AS A DISTRACTION, TURN TO PAGE 72.
- IF YOU WANT TO STAY HIDDEN, TURN TO PAGE 74.

You don't know how long you'll have to hide, so you might as well pick somewhere with snacks! You enter the snack bar, passing the empty tables and going over to the ordering counter. Like the mini golf course, everything here is Monty-themed, with images of the rock and roll alligator everywhere, awash in green and purple lighting. There's fake greenery scattered about as well, though nothing big enough to hide behind. There are the counter and the kitchen, though, both of which look promising. Maybe in the kitchen you can cook yourself up an order of the "swamp fries" on the menu, which you hope are more appetizing than they sound.

Except . . .

You don't know how long a head start Monty is giving you. Gregory is probably hiding already, and you don't want to give him the satisfaction of being caught before you've even had a chance to hide. But the area seems empty for the moment, so maybe you have a few minutes to explore the snack bar further?

- **IF YOU WANT TO SEARCH THE SNACK BAR AREA FURTHER BEFORE HIDING, TURN TO PAGE 75.**
- **IF YOU WANT TO GRAB A QUICK SNACK AND HUNKER DOWN RIGHT NOW, TURN TO PAGE 77.**

Monty is acting weird enough that you want to observe him further. Maybe if you do, you can figure out what's wrong with him. You creep forward slowly, thankful that the soft tongue of the giant gator head swallows your steps. You get closer to the front of the mouth, crouching down so you're still partially hidden by the row of teeth.

Monty is a little way away, stomping around the course with the golf club clenched in one fist. He's still twitching and acting increasingly strange—continuing to talk to himself, low, so you can't make out the words. But he doesn't sound happy.

Suddenly, a security bot, drawn by the smashed hole marker, comes rolling up to investigate. Monty twists around suddenly and lets out a loud growl. He lunges at the security bot, which doesn't seem to understand the danger as Monty raises the golf club and swings it. There are loud clanging noises as it connects, again and again and again. Within moments, Monty has reduced the security bot to a twitching pile of metal and wires.

That's *definitely* not right. Panic grips you, and before you realize it, you're running, leaping out of the gator's head and bolting across the river bridges.

Too late, you realize your mistake.

"There you are!" Monty screeches. His stomping tread seems to rattle the whole course as he pursues you.

"Help!" you cry, heading for the stairs, which seem much farther away than a few minutes ago. "Help, Gregory! Monty's gone crazy!"

You make it to the stairs, but you can hear Monty close behind. A heavy, clawed hand grabs you before you've made it halfway up, and you're suddenly in free fall as Monty yanks you back down to the fake grass of the mini golf course.

A shadow falls over you. All you can see are two enraged eyes and lots and lots of teeth.

You scream as Monty's snout descends.

Then, he stops. Through your tears, you see that Monty has gone limp, the rage in his face gone.

"Cassie?"

You twist around and jump to your feet. On the stairs above stands Gregory, tapping at his device.

"That wasn't funny!" you cry. "You promised no more jokes."

"It wasn't a joke!" He almost—*almost*—sounds sincere. "I don't know what happened. Something in Monty's programming must have glitched!"

You cross your arms, sure he's suppressing laughter. But Gregory isn't laughing this time. Maybe he's telling the truth.

"I'll figure it out," he promises. "I'll fix it."

You're not sure you believe him.

➤ TURN TO PAGE 88.

Whatever is going on with Monty, it's definitely not right. Maybe it's another one of Gregory's pranks?

Or maybe not.

Either way, you're not willing to let Monty catch you. Luckily, you have just the thing to use as a distraction. You reach into your bag and pull out the jar of screws and bolts that you found on Roxy Raceway. You creep to the edge of the gator mouth and reach out. If you roll it, aim it just right . . .

You toss the jar of screws and bolts. It lands on one of the holes, rattling as it rolls down an incline toward the river. Monty goes stiff as he hears the noise and turns toward it. A moment later he snarls and runs, ready to tear apart the source of the sound.

You turn and bolt in the opposite direction. Running as fast as you can, you make it to the top of the stairs before you hear an angry cry below.

"I'm gonna get you!" Your distraction didn't last long. In a flash, Monty is chasing after you, and he is *fast*.

"Help!" you cry as you run toward the Pizzaplex lobby, the sound of Monty's footsteps getting closer and closer. "Help, Gregory! Where are you? Something is wrong with Monty!"

You burst out of Gator Golf but only make it a few more steps before a clawed hand grabs your arm and jerks you backward. You scream as you land on the tile floor, skidding across it. A few steps away, Monty watches you, licking his lips. He bares his teeth in a snarl.

"Ready or not . . ." His head twitches to one side, eyes alight and angry. "Oh, yeah, you're not ready."

There's nothing you can do. You close your eyes.

Heartbeats pass.

Nothing happens.

You open your eyes again to find that Monty has stopped barely a step away. He's gone limp, somehow deactivated. Then, you see Gregory. He's standing behind Monty, a device in hand.

"Not funny!" You jump to your feet and stomp toward him, jabbing a finger his way. "You promised no more jokes!"

"It wasn't a joke!" Gregory says.

You glare at him, suspicious.

"I swear," he insists. "Something went wrong with Monty's programming."

Monty was acting super strange, twitching and stuff. Part of you wonders if Gregory is telling the truth.

But only part.

"Whatever it was," Gregory continues, "I'll fix it. Before tomorrow night."

Even if he does, you think to yourself, you're done with hide-and-seek.

➤ **TURN TO PAGE 88.**

Whatever is wrong with Monty, it's got you too scared to risk revealing yourself. You keep to the shadows within the giant gator head as the noises outside of it grow louder and more frantic. You can hear Monty muttering to himself, but you can't make out what he's saying. There are crashes and clangs, and every few minutes Monty stomps into view, twitching and stumbling as he makes his way around the course.

You hold your breath, a cold sensation growing in your stomach. This has to be another prank, right? Another one of Gregory's "games." And yet, no matter how hard you try to convince yourself of this, you can't manage to be brave and confront Monty, or even make a run for it. Instead, you scrunch yourself down among the gator teeth, hoping that it's as dark from the outside as it seems on the inside.

Slowly, the noises start to get quieter. Then, they stop. You hope Monty has moved along to another area of the Pizzaplex, so you can go find Gregory. Find out if this is a joke, or if something really is wrong with Monty.

You're just about to summon the courage to sneak out and make sure Monty is gone when you hear his footsteps again. He stomps into view, stopping directly in front of the gator mouth. Slowly, his head turns your way, twitching once before going still. Then: his eyes light up.

They shine directly onto you.

"I found you," Monty says, moving forward and blocking all chance at escape. In the faint light, all you can see are eyes. And teeth.

You have only a moment to understand that this isn't a joke before Monty strikes.

GAME OVER

> TO START FROM THE BEGINNING, TURN TO PAGE 3.
> TO TRY THIS NIGHT AGAIN, TURN TO PAGE 48.

You can't resist the temptation to check out the snack bar further. Going around the counter, you peek into the kitchen area behind the snack bar. To your disappointment, there's nothing very interesting. The usual food production machines, all shut down for the night. The only place to hide in here would be the industrial-sized fridge, and you don't feel like being cold while Monty searches for you.

Giving up, you start to go back out to the front counter when something on the floor catches your eye. The edge of a card is sticking out from beneath one of the prep tables. You pick it up: It's a food service key card. It doesn't seem like it will do much good for you in Gator Golf, but you keep it anyway, adding it to your bag in case it will come in handy later. Then, you push through the kitchen area door, going back out to the front counter.

Immediately, you freeze. There are noises approaching, and a chuffing sound that can only be Monty himself. You have to hide quick!

There aren't many options. The best you can see (that's quick and close) is the snack bar counter. Not a great spot, but you don't have a choice. Monty is getting nearer. You duck beneath it as the footsteps approach, wedging yourself in among the shelves of snacks as quietly as possible.

Monty is extremely close now. You can hear the heavy tread of his steps. But you can't see anything from behind the counter. Eventually you can hear muttering, too. Definitely Monty's voice, but you can't make out what he's saying. Only that it sounds . . . odd.

After a minute or so, Monty seems to move on. It gets quiet again; at least, as quiet as the Gator Golf ever is. You almost wish Monty would do something loud, so you'd know if he's still close. Your hiding place isn't exactly comfortable, and if he's gone, it might be a good idea to find a better one!

- ADD FOOD SERVICE KEY CARD TO YOUR INVENTORY. IF YOU WANT TO STAY HIDDEN UNDER THE SNACK BAR COUNTER, TURN TO PAGE 78.
- ADD FOOD SERVICE KEY CARD TO YOUR INVENTORY. IF YOU WANT TO PEEK OUT AND SEE IF MONTY IS GONE SO YOU CAN FIND ANOTHER HIDING SPOT, TURN TO PAGE 79.

You're not letting Gregory beat you at this game. Which means you're not going to risk Monty coming in without you having found a good hiding spot!

There's a corner behind the snack bar counter, which wouldn't be a great spot normally, but there are some boxes nearby that, if you pull them closer, will cover you. And even better: There are a bunch of snacks behind the counter. You grab a bag of chips and then wedge yourself into the space, pulling the boxes over until you have a perfect spot. No way Monty will notice you here!

Then, you wait. It's kind of boring, and your hiding spot gets less comfortable over time, but you don't mind. The longer you can hold out, the more likely Monty will find Gregory first. You're just beginning to feel hungry enough to open the chips when there are noises nearby. Footsteps, heavy ones, and then growling. It's Monty for sure. You can hear him talking.

"Gonna find . . . look here look there . . . find you and then . . ."

But who is he talking to?

You strain your ears, but whatever Monty is muttering doesn't seem to make sense. And every so often, a word just . . . cuts off. A moment later, the muttering continues.

Which seems . . . strange.

"GONNA FIND YOU!" Monty suddenly screams, making you jump. You hold your breath. Is this another one of Gregory's jokes? Is he having Monty act weird so that you'll get scared again? If it is another prank, you're going to give Gregory a piece of your mind.

But what if it's not?

The muttering continues, and you're not sure what to do. Should you peek out and see what Monty is doing? Or stay hidden and hope he passes, then go find Gregory and see if this is just another mean game?

➤ IF YOU WANT TO PEEK OUT AND OBSERVE MONTY, TURN TO PAGE 80.

➤ IF YOU WANT TO WAIT UNTIL MONTY HAS MOVED ON AND THEN FIND GREGORY, TURN TO PAGE 81.

The way Monty is acting, you don't want to risk him finding you there, so you remain hidden behind the snack bar. From down on the course, you can still hear noises. Monty is stomping around, muttering as he does.

Bang!

Suddenly, you hear a crash as if something has been broken. A squeak escapes you, and you slap a hand over your mouth, even though Monty must be too far away to hear you. More smashing sounds follow, along with Monty's growls.

This must be another joke of Gregory's, right? But given the danger and destruction, you're not sure you're willing to risk it. You decide not to wait around and give Monty a chance to find you. *You* are going to find Gregory, and if he's pulling another prank on you, you're going to be furious. But you have to escape Gator Golf first, which means eluding Monty. He's still on the course, so your best chance is now.

But should you make a break for it and run, giving Monty the chance to find you? Or crawl your way out of the mini golf area, which will be slower but less risky?

The crashing continues, and you need to decide.

➤ **IF YOU WANT TO RUN BACK INTO THE PIZZAPLEX, TURN TO PAGE 82.**

➤ **IF YOU CRAWL YOUR WAY OUT OF MONTY'S GATOR GOLF, TURN TO PAGE 84.**

You're not exactly sure what's going on with Monty, but your hiding spot is definitely not as good as you'd like it to be. If you move fast, you should be able to find a better one. But first you need to make sure that Monty is far enough away that he won't spot you.

You creep to the end of the snack bar and peek around. You can't see much of the mini golf course from here, only the rest of the snack bar and the stairs down. A lone cleaning bot is rolling around near the exit into the Pizzaplex. You wish you knew exactly where Monty is at the moment, but from the sound of it, he was heading down to the course. This is your chance to get out of here!

Staying low, you come out from behind the snack counter, keeping an eye on the cleaning bot. The last thing you need is it spotting you and alerting Monty to your presence. But the coast looks clear now.

You're just about to bolt for the exit when the sound of heavy chuffing comes from behind.

"Found you." You turn. Monty has snuck up behind you. He's staring down, strangely blank-eyed. Every few seconds, his head twitches. "You know what that means, right?"

You take a wary step back. "Okay, Monty, you found me. I give up. Gregory wins."

His eyes narrow. "Wrong. It means YOU LOSE."

Before you can run, Monty grabs you, claws digging into you as he lifts you off the ground.

All you can do is scream.

GAME OVER

➤ TO START FROM THE BEGINNING, TURN TO PAGE 3.
➤ TO TRY THIS NIGHT AGAIN, TURN TO PAGE 48.

Monty sounds weird, but you need to see what's going on with him. Carefully, and as quietly as you can, you slide the boxes around a little so you have room to climb out. In the distance, you can still hear Monty, stomping around and muttering. *This must be another one of Gregory's pranks. He probably told Monty to act this way to scare me.* You're not going to let him fool you this time, though. If Monty is putting on an act, you can figure it out.

As you climb out from behind the counter, you forget about your snack. The bag of chips, wedged between you and the wall, suddenly pops. You wince at the noise, hoping Monty is too far away to hear.

But no such luck.

"I hear you!" Monty's stomping footsteps come heading for you. You get to your feet, trying to make it around the counter and run for the exit, but it's too late. Monty is right in front of you.

You're cornered.

"Found you," Monty growls.

You take a step back. But you do your best not to look scared. "I give up," you say.

Monty growls again, teeth bared. His eyes narrow. "I found you," he says again, lower.

A cold sensation runs up your spine. "R-r-right," you stutter. "Gregory wins . . . I lose."

"Yes." Monty comes forward, teeth growing larger and larger as he gets closer. *"You lose."*

GAME OVER

> TO START FROM THE BEGINNING, TURN TO PAGE 3.

> TO TRY THIS NIGHT AGAIN, TURN TO PAGE 48.

This has to be another one of Gregory's games. And you don't feel like playing it. You're going to wait until Monty has gone, then you're going to go find Gregory. By now he must have picked out a hiding place in Bonnie Bowl. You don't care if you ruin the game, you're going to find him there and make him tell you what's going on with Monty.

You wait, wedged in underneath the snack counter, with the boxes beside you, until you can't hear Monty anymore. You aren't sure if that means he's down on the course somewhere on the opposite end of Gator Golf or if he's left the area all together. Either way, if you can't hear him, this might be a good chance to sneak away.

But what if there is something wrong with Monty? You haven't seen him so far, and even if you find Gregory, what are you going to tell him? Minutes tick by as you consider what to do. On one hand, you could go straight to Bonnie Bowl, flush out Gregory from wherever he is hiding, and let him figure out what's going on. On the other, he might think you're a scaredy-cat for running away so easily. And that's what he was doing with Freddy, wasn't he? Trying to scare you?

Maybe you should stay here a little longer and observe Monty, so you have something real to report back to Gregory.

- **IF YOU GO STRAIGHT TO BONNIE BOWL TO FIND GREGORY, TURN TO PAGE 85.**
- **IF YOU DECIDE TO OBSERVE MONTY A LITTLE LONGER IN GATOR GOLF, TURN TO PAGE 86.**

Your best chance to escape is now, and you're going to take it. You crawl out from beneath the counter and creep to the end of it. You can hear Monty down on the course, still stomping around.

"I'm going to find you!" he screeches, and the furious sound of his voice is what gets you moving. You jump up and dash forward, not caring if you're visible as you sprint across the snack bar area and toward the exit. In your haste, you hit a chair as you pass, overturning it with a *crash*. You wince, but don't slow. If Monty didn't know you were there before, he does now!

"There you are! GONNA GET YOU, CASSIE!"

Your heart rises into your throat when you hear Monty yell your name. You know you shouldn't, but you glance back over your shoulder. Monty is flying up the stairs, eyes burning with anger. His movements are uneven and twitchy, but that doesn't appear to be slowing him down. In fact, he's gaining on you!

"Help!"

You run for the Gator Golf lobby as Monty's steps get closer. You can hear him growling, nearly on the back of your neck.

You can't help it. You scream.

"Help!" You burst out of Gator Golf and back into the Pizzaplex lobby. "Gregory! Where are you? Something is wrong with Monty!"

You barely get the words out before a clawed hand snaps down on your shoulder. You trip, but Monty grabs you before you fall, lifting you off your feet and twisting you around.

Teeth. All you can see is teeth. The heat coming off his glitching circuits hits your face, and you freeze. You can't fight. Monty is too strong.

"Caught you . . ." Monty says with a low growl.

All you can do is close your eyes.

Then, suddenly, you drop. Your feet hit the floor and you stumble backward, nearly falling.

"Cassie?" Gregory stands a few feet away, a device in hand. "Are you okay?"

At first, you can't speak. "That wasn't funny!" you finally spit out. "You promised no more jokes."

Wide-eyed, Gregory shakes his head. "It wasn't a joke. I don't know what happened. Something with Monty's programming—it must have glitched."

He seems truthful, but sometimes, with Gregory, it's hard to tell. "He was twitching, acting really weird."

He nods as if that makes sense. "Must have been an error. I'll fix it before tomorrow night."

You cross your arms, but don't say anything. Fixed or not, you're not sure you want to play any more of Gregory's games.

➤ **TURN TO PAGE 88.**

You're too afraid to run and reveal to Monty that you're here. Instead, you wait until it sounds like he is on the far end of the course. Then, staying low, you crawl out from behind the snack bar counter, making your way across the sitting area and toward the Gator Golf lobby. Below, on the course, Monty continues to mutter and growl every few seconds, and soon there's another crashing sound. Still, crawling seems to be working. Monty can't see you, and the exit through the mini golf lobby is growing closer.

Suddenly, a cleaning bot rolls out of the lobby. It spots you and starts to make a shrill noise, as if you're a mess and it wants to clean you up.

"Shhhh," you hiss, but it's too late.

"WHO'S THERE?!" Monty yells.

You jump up and try to run, but the bot gets in your way. Shoving past it, you run for the exit. You're almost there when a clawed hand clamps down on your shoulder. You scream as Monty violently twists you around, lifting you up like you weigh nothing. Monty, chuffing heavily, tightens his grip.

"Found you, Cassie," he growls. You're close enough to see every single one of his teeth. "You lose."

You want to scream again, but it freezes in your throat.

All you can do is close your eyes.

GAME OVER

➤ TO START FROM THE BEGINNING, TURN TO PAGE 3.

➤ TO TRY THIS NIGHT AGAIN, TURN TO PAGE 48.

Moving slowly and silently, you slide the boxes aside so you can climb out of your hiding spot, then creep to the end of the snack bar and around it. You take care as you peek out, but from what you can see, Gator Golf looks deserted.

Then you hear a *crash*.

From down on the course, you suddenly sense Monty again, sounding angrier than ever. You sneak as close to the rail as you dare, just barely able to see his hulking form in the distance. Monty has picked up a putter and, as you watch, he brings it down, smashing one of the hole markers.

You've seen enough. If something is up with Monty, you're going to leave it to Gregory to figure out. Staying quiet, you head for the exit to the Pizzaplex as the crashing and muttering continues behind you. But the moment you reach the lobby, a cleaning bot suddenly appears. Its appearance surprises you so much that you stumble back, knocking over a fake plant. It tumbles over, knocking over several others as it falls.

"I hear you!" Monty cries.

Your heart jumps into your throat, and you try to run, but the cleaning bot keeps getting in front of you, blocking your way. Finally, you shove your way past it. But you can hear Monty running after you.

"I see you!" He sounds far too close. But you don't waste time looking back. You bolt into the atrium and toward Bonnie Bowl. You're halfway there when you trip, sprawling across the carpet. Twisting around, you try to get to your feet, but Monty is already above you. He descends, teeth bared.

You have just enough time to understand that this isn't another prank.

GAME OVER

➤ TO START FROM THE BEGINNING, TURN TO PAGE 3.

➤ TO TRY THIS NIGHT AGAIN, TURN TO PAGE 48.

You're not a scaredy-cat. And you're not going to go running to Gregory with nothing more than a speculation that "Monty is acting weird." He'll probably just laugh at you. If there *is* something wrong with Monty, you need to figure it out before you go running for Bonnie Bowl.

Staying low, you creep over to the rail of the stairs overlooking the mini golf course. Luckily, Monty has his back to you as he stomps around. He's carrying a putter and, as you watch, he raises it and smashes one of the hole markers before continuing his sweep of the course. You can hear his muttering better now, but it's mostly nonsensical, and his movements are jerky and sharp. At one point, he seems to freeze, then twitches and lets out a low growl before using the club to destroy a plant.

Your stomach drops. This could still be a prank. But intuition tells you that something is actually wrong, and that Monty is malfunctioning in some way. And whatever way that is, you're not waiting around to find out!

You turn to leave when your foot knocks against something. You look down in time to see a stray golf ball roll away . . . directly for the stairs! You lunge to grab it, but it's too late. It rolls down the stairs, plunking loudly against each step as it goes.

Monty turns in a flash, spotting you. "I found you!" he yells and runs straight for you.

You take off bolting for the mini golf lobby. But Monty is faster than you. You can hear him as he climbs the stairs, heavy steps getting closer and closer with each passing moment.

"Help!" you yell at the top of your lungs as you run. "Gregory, help!"

You make it to the Pizzaplex lobby, getting halfway across before Monty grabs you. You scream again.

"Found you!" Monty snaps, jaws inches from your face. "You lose!"

You can't fight. Monty is too strong.

Then, suddenly, the animatronic freezes. You push away, freeing yourself and falling to the floor as you hear your name.

"Cassie?" It's Gregory. He stands a few feet away, tapping at his display. "What happened?"

Heart still pounding, you get to your feet. "Monty went wild! Is this another one of your jokes?"

Gregory shakes his head. "No, I swear. Something . . . something must have gone wrong with his programming."

You glare at him, but he seems to be telling the truth . . . maybe. "He was acting all twitchy, smashing stuff."

Gregory peers at his device. "Must be a glitch. I'll figure it out and fix it before tomorrow night," he promises.

This you believe. Not that it matters.

You're getting very tired of Gregory's games.

➤ TURN TO PAGE 88.

NIGHT 3

It always feels a little weird, being in the Pizzaplex when it's actually open and full of people. The crowds have started to thin out as closing time approaches and your third overnight adventure begins, but there are still plenty of families milling about, playing games, picking out prizes, and scarfing down the last of their popcorn and pizza. You're lingering with Gregory in a remote corner, watching as Freddy lumbers about the lobby, waving and snapping selfies with kids. If only they knew how much fun the Pizzaplex could be at night, when you have it all to yourself.

At least, it *used* to be fun. The last two nights have left a terrible feeling in the pit of your stomach, nervous about whatever Gregory has in store. He swears he's fixed the problem with Monty, but you're not sure you believe him. In fact, you're not sure there was a problem to begin with. Maybe it was an intentional "glitch" added by Gregory. His games have been getting so serious lately. So . . . real. If they are this dangerous, are they really games at all?

Gregory is watching the people trickle out, anticipation blooming on his features. You're not sure you want to know what he has in store for tonight.

In fact, you know you don't.

"I'm gonna go," you say.

His attention snaps over to you, mouth turning downward into a frown. "What?"

"I said, I'm going to go." You start toward the door. "I don't feel like playing tonight."

"Cassie, wait!" he calls after you. "Don't go!"

But you don't listen. You stalk off, determined to stick to your decision. Maybe if he doesn't have anyone to play with for a night or two, Gregory will learn his lesson. As you reach where Freddy stands, the animatronic suddenly steps into your path.

"Hey, Cassie!" Freddy says too cheerily. "Where you going?"

"Sorry, Freddy." You try to go around him. "No games tonight."

Freddy holds out an arm, blocking you. "But you can't leave."

"What?" You take a step back. "But I—"

You don't get a chance to say more. Freddy grabs you, scooping you into his chest cavity, which closes up before you have a chance to fight back.

"Hey!" You bang your fists against Freddy's insides. "Hey, Freddy, stop it! Gregory, help! This isn't funny!"

But Freddy doesn't budge. And no matter how much you yell and bang and beg, no one answers your cries.

Hours pass before Freddy's chest opens up again. Gregory peers in before he backs away, allowing you a chance to escape the chamber. You tumble to the floor of Freddy's greenroom.

"Gregory!" You're so mad you don't know where to start. You jump to your feet, hands balled into fists. "Why are you being so mean? I can't believe you—"

"Cassie, I didn't do anything!" Gregory throws up his hands, face tight with apprehension. "It was all Freddy!"

"I don't believe you," you snap. You take a deep breath and let it out. Why are you bothering? You turn on your heel, ready to make for the exit. If Gregory thinks you're sticking around to play after this, he's got another thing coming!

But Freddy grabs your arm, holding you back. "It's true, Cassie. I'm sorry, but I had to keep you safe."

"Safe?" After the last two nights, it doesn't seem like your safety matters to Gregory or Freddy. "What are you talking about?"

"I'm afraid the Pizzaplex is being . . ." Freddy pauses, thinking. "Cleaned."

You aren't sure what Freddy means, but you don't like the sound of it. "Gregory?"

He nods. "The Pizzaplex has activated a Reagent. It's sweeping the whole Pizzaplex, getting rid of all the organic matter."

Like you and Gregory. Your stomach clenches.

"I think Freddy and I can stop it," Gregory continues. "But we need to get you somewhere safe while we work."

You're wary. This sounds like the setup for another prank. "Where?"

"The kitchen," Gregory says. "We can hide you in there and focus on stopping the Reagent."

Still nervous, you follow Gregory and Freddy to the main kitchen, where all the food machines have been shut down for the night. It's dark, and what little light follows you inside glints sharply off the stainless-steel counters and shelves. Despite being a kitchen, the only signs of food are stacks of boxes and cans, all sealed and neatly organized. The room smells more like cleaning supplies than anything you could possibly eat.

"Wait here," Gregory instructs. "Keep out of sight until we come back and tell you it's safe."

With that, Gregory and Freddy rush off, leaving you in the metallic dark. For a minute, you just stand there, not sure what to do.

You don't know if you can trust Gregory.

But if he's telling the truth, and there is a dangerous bot roaming the Pizzaplex, you should find a place to hide. Or some protection, at least.

Whatever you do, you should make a decision soon.

- **IF YOU WANT TO FIND A PLACE IN THE KITCHEN TO HIDE, TURN TO PAGE 91.**
- **IF YOU WANT TO EXPLORE THE KITCHEN FURTHER AND LOOK FOR A WAY TO PROTECT YOURSELF, TURN TO PAGE 92.**
- **IF YOU WANT TO FOLLOW GREGORY AND MAKE SURE THIS ISN'T ANOTHER ONE OF HIS PRANKS, TURN TO PAGE 93.**

Gregory may not be telling the truth, but if there is a bot that can make short work of all the organic matter in the Pizzaplex, you don't want to find out! You decide to trust Gregory—despite his tendency toward tricks and pranks—and find a place in the kitchen to hide. Wandering through it, you inspect your options. There's no shortage of them in the sprawling room. Beneath the worktables there are tons of cabinets, and full shelves line the wall, several of which look like you could squeeze behind. You check some of the cabinets. Most are full of pots and pans and all sorts of cooking equipment, but a few are empty enough to allow you to climb inside.

Wary, you glance back at the doors to the kitchen, and the porthole windows set in them. Did a shadow just pass by? You shake your head. Gregory's warning is getting to you. The kitchen is deserted, and you can't hear anything nearby, either.

Still, you shouldn't wait to find yourself a good place to hole up until Gregory and Freddy come back.

➤ **IF YOU WANT TO HIDE IN A CABINET, TURN TO PAGE 94.**
➤ **IF YOU HIDE BEHIND ONE OF THE SHELVES, TURN TO PAGE 95.**

Gregory said to hide, but after the last two nights, you'd feel better if you had protection of some kind. Even though you're not sure the Reagent actually exists, you begin looking around the kitchen. The room is sprawling and dark, and eerily quiet compared to during the day, when it would be bustling with service bots making pizza and hot dogs to feed the hungry Pizzaplex patrons. It's so big that, if Gregory is telling the truth, you may not have the time to spend searching everywhere.

There are a lot of counters, with a lot of prep equipment. There are also dozens of cabinets that might hold something you can defend yourself with. And, tucked in the back, there's a walk-in refrigerator. Who knows what you might find in there? You glance back at the kitchen door, unsure of what to do, but knowing that whatever it is, you should do it soon.

➤ **IF YOU WANT TO SEARCH THE FRIDGE, TURN TO PAGE 100.**
➤ **IF YOU WANT TO SEARCH THE CABINETS, TURN TO PAGE 101.**
➤ **IF YOU WANT TO SEARCH THE COUNTERS, TURN TO PAGE 102.**

After Gregory and Freddy leave, you just stand for a moment, still in shock. The kitchen is silent and dark, even more so with them gone, and you don't like the idea of being stuck here until Gregory decides to return. Also, you can't shake the feeling that this is another joke being played on you. After the last two nights, you wouldn't put anything past Gregory.

But why would he leave you in the kitchen, of all places? Maybe he *is* telling the truth and there is a dangerous bot on the loose in the Pizzaplex. The last thing you want is to run into something like that, but . . .

No—you can't trust Gregory. You decide to follow him and Freddy, and see what they are up to.

You go over to the kitchen doors, but when you try to push them open, they don't budge. They're locked! Frustrated, you push harder, but it's no use. You're stuck. You play with the keypad a little, but it looks like the only way you're going to get the door unlocked is to use a key card.

- **IF YOU HAVE A <u>FOOD SERVICE KEY CARD</u>, TURN TO PAGE 110.**
- **IF YOU WANT TO FIND A PLACE IN THE KITCHEN TO HIDE, TURN TO PAGE 91.**
- **IF YOU WANT TO EXPLORE THE KITCHEN FURTHER AND LOOK FOR A WAY TO PROTECT YOURSELF, TURN TO PAGE 92.**

As much as you don't relish the idea of hiding in the dark, you decide that one of the cabinets is the best place to hide in the kitchen. You pick an empty one that faces the direction of the kitchen door. That way, if you crack the cabinet open, you can see if anyone—or *anything*—comes inside. You crouch down and fold yourself into the space, barely getting comfortable before you hear a *creak*.

The door to the kitchen is opening.

You quickly pull the cabinet shut . . . mostly. You have to know what's coming in. You expect Gregory or Freddy, trying to sneak up on you as part of a joke; instead, a bot you've never seen before crawls in. It doesn't look friendly or helpful, like the other service bots in the Pizzaplex; no, this bot is bigger than usual, with blank, glassy eyes that remind you of an insect. There are tanks attached to its back, and its "arms" end in nozzle attachments.

Your stomach does a flip. Gregory was telling the truth.

Holding your breath, you watch as the Reagent makes its way into the kitchen, its head swiveling and searching, scanning the room. Slowly, it gets closer.

Then it stops, right outside your cabinet. Only the thinnest sliver of it is visible. Your heart pounds as it pauses there.

It finally moves on, out of your view. You can still hear the faint knocking of its treads against the tile floor, but the sound grows fainter and fainter until you hear nothing. You wait, barely daring to breathe, but minutes pass without any change. Did the Reagent finish searching the kitchen and move on? You want to look out to see if it's gone, but if it's not . . . maybe you should stay hidden instead.

➤ **IF YOU WANT TO PEEK OUT AND SEE IF THE REAGENT IS GONE, TURN TO PAGE 96.**

➤ **IF YOU REMAIN HIDDEN IN THE CABINET, TURN TO PAGE 97.**

Hiding in the cabinets is tempting, but too obvious, so you decide to hide behind the shelves instead. That way, you'll have a full view of the kitchen. You go over to one of the racks of canned tomato sauce for the pizza. It's set a little away from the wall, giving you enough space to slip behind. It's a tight fit, but you make it, picking a spot that allows you to see between the cans. From the other side, though, you'll be almost invisible.

Then, you wait.

And wait.

Finally, so much time passes that you're sure this is another prank. Maybe instead of trying to scare you tonight, Gregory is trying to bore you to death. You sigh, shifting to lean against the wall, tempted to go search for Gregory and Freddy. The more minutes tick by, the more you're sure that they are somewhere playing games without you.

Then, suddenly, the door to the kitchen creaks.

You stiffen as it opens and a bot rolls in. It's not like any you've seen before. It's bigger, with insect-like eyes on a head that swivels rapidly around the kitchen, searching. Two "arms" end in nozzles, with hoses that lead into the tanks on its back.

You suck in a breath. Gregory wasn't lying. This must be the Reagent.

Slowly, deliberately, it makes its way through the kitchen. You press against the wall, holding your breath as it draws closer. Then, it's right in front of your shelves, so close you could reach out and touch it.

It pauses. Searching.

Then, to your relief, it keeps moving.

You can't stay where you are. Any second, the Reagent is going to spot you—you just know it. Maybe you can cause a distraction, make a run for it? Or sneak out and hide in one of the cabinets instead? Leaning against the wall to brace yourself, you try to decide what to do.

- **IF YOU HAVE A <u>CAN OF SODARONI</u> TO CREATE A DISTRACTION WITH, TURN TO PAGE 98.**
- **IF YOU SNEAK OUT AND HIDE IN A CABINET, TURN TO PAGE 99.**

More time passes, and you can't keep still any longer. You have to know if the Reagent is gone. Moving slowly, you open the cabinet door another inch, peering out. A little more of the kitchen becomes visible, but no matter how you strain, you can't see the bot anywhere nearby. So, you open the door a little more.

Suddenly, there's a hissing sound. You pull back as quickly as you can, but only inches away the Reagent passes in front of the cabinet. A noxious cloud follows in its wake, the thick, sharp scent of chemicals filling your nostrils. You reach for the cabinet, intending to run for the kitchen door, but within moments, your vision wavers.

There's just enough time for you to hope this is a prank before everything goes dark.

GAME OVER

➤ TO START FROM THE BEGINNING, TURN TO PAGE 3.
➤ TO TRY THIS NIGHT AGAIN, TURN TO PAGE 88.

It seems like a bad idea to risk checking the kitchen to see if the Reagent is gone, so instead, you opt to *hope* it's gone, but stay hidden in the cabinet. In fact, you pull the door shut entirely. Darkness swallows you, so thick that the rest of your senses strain for any clues of where the Reagent might be. You think you can hear little noises, hints of something moving around, but for all you know, your fear might be playing tricks on you. You hug your knees to your chest, hoping whatever Gregory and Freddy are doing works, and quickly!

Suddenly, you hear something. You're sure of it this time—the Reagent is moving, and from the sound of it, it's right outside your cabinet! Worse, there's a hissing sound as well. You're not sure what it is . . . not until the smell hits you. Sharp. Burning. Your heart leaps into your chest as you realize the Reagent has released its chemicals. You pull your shirt up over your face, holding your breath, but it doesn't matter. In the darkness, a sense of vertigo overtakes you.

Then: light.

A square of illumination opens in your vision: the cabinet door, flung open. You try to scream, but the chemicals are choking you. It's not the Reagent that appears.

It's Roxanne Wolf.

You smile, despite the chemicals, and try to say her name, but everything is becoming fuzzy. Roxy reaches for you.

Then, everything goes dark.

➤ **TURN TO PAGE 118.**

If you can distract the Reagent, you can make a run for it, and find Gregory and Freddy. They'll be able to help. You rack your brain for a way to turn the Reagent's attention away from the door . . . and then it hits you—you have a can of Sodaroni! You pull it out of your bag and give it a healthy shake. Then, you slide carefully to the end of the shelves and get ready. The Reagent is making its way between the long metal kitchen tables, still searching for any trace of organic matter.

Perfect.

You crack the tab of the Sodaroni, just a little, then roll it down the aisle. It hisses like a snake, sending out a thin spray of soda. Immediately, the Reagent swivels toward it, and you take your chance! You burst from behind the shelves and run, heading for the kitchen door. It's not far, but with all the counters, the kitchen feels almost like a maze.

You're fast, but not fast enough. Though the soda initially draws its attention, the Reagent twists your way at the sound of your footsteps, its buggy eyes zeroing in. There's a new hissing sound, this time louder, as the Reagent sets off its gases. A chemical smell fills your nostrils, burning them.

But you can still make it.

The doors aren't far. You keep going, stumbling as the world goes fuzzy. But you can make it . . . you can make it . . .

The last thing you see is the floor rushing up at you.

Then: nothing.

GAME OVER

➤ TO START FROM THE BEGINNING, TURN TO PAGE 3.

➤ TO TRY THIS NIGHT AGAIN, TURN TO PAGE 88.

Your hiding place is suddenly feeling a lot less secure. The Reagent doesn't seem to be checking the cabinets, so you decide to sneak out and hide in one of them. You wait until the Reagent is all the way across the kitchen, then slide along the wall to the end of the shelf. Keeping a close eye on it, you crouch down and carefully make your way over to the nearest counter, opening the cabinet at the end. Luckily, there's enough room inside for you to fit. You make your way in, closing the door behind you. You're plunged into complete darkness and you wait, heart thudding, expecting the Reagent to pull the door open at any moment and discover you.

That fear grips harder as you hear it rolling closer, closer . . .

Then, it stops . . . right outside your cabinet. You hold your breath, but a moment later it keeps going, and you exhale, relieved.

Until you hear the hissing.

Suddenly, a sharp chemical smell creeps into the air, burning your nostrils. It may not have found you, but the Reagent released its chemicals anyway! You pull your shirt up, trying not to breathe, your eyes watering.

It's too late. Dizziness grips you.

Suddenly, the door flies open. You blink. There's something large outside it, but it's not the Reagent. The form leans down and a face appears.

Your favorite face.

Roxy reaches for you as darkness swirls at the edges of your vision and takes over.

➤ **TURN TO PAGE 118.**

You decide to head to the fridge first; it's the only place where you won't have a view of the kitchen doors while you search. You pull the handle and the door swings open, a blast of chilly air hitting you in the face. Inside, the walls are lined with shelves. There isn't that much real food to see, mostly cartons of batter, packaged toppings, and a box of hot dogs. You pick up a block of packaged cheese that looks more like plastic than food. Maybe it wouldn't hurt for the Pizzaplex to add a vegetable or two to its menu?

But you're not going to be able to defend yourself with hot dogs or cheese. You search a little more, but disappointment grows as you find nothing interesting. Then, just as you are about to leave, something cylindrical beneath one of the shelves catches your eye. It's a screwdriver. You're not sure why it's in the refrigerator, but you decide to take it. Who knows, maybe it will come in handy later?

- ADD SCREWDRIVER TO YOUR INVENTORY. IF YOU WANT TO SEARCH THE CABINETS, TURN TO PAGE 101.
- ADD SCREWDRIVER TO YOUR INVENTORY. IF YOU WANT TO SEARCH THE COUNTERS, TURN TO PAGE 102.

There are cabinets running beneath all the long kitchen counters, and if you are going to find anything useful, that's where it's going to be. You start at the nearest one, pulling open door after door. Some are empty. Others have cooking equipment in them, and supplies to make all the Pizzaplex's snacks, like boxes of pizza dough mix. But no matter how many cabinets you search through, you can't find anything that you might use to defend yourself. Gregory should have picked somewhere better to stash you!

Then again, you're still not even sure he's telling the truth. Maybe this is a prank, too, a bad one, where you spend the whole night in the kitchen, bored to—

You freeze as you hear a creaking sound. Crouching down, you watch as the kitchen doors open slowly and a bot rolls in. It's not like any you've ever seen before. It's big, all dark gray metal and blank, buggy eyes that search the kitchen as it moves. Two "arms" end in nozzles, and you see tanks attached to the bot's back.

This must be the Reagent bot.

Gregory was telling the truth!

Your heart pounds as the bot moves farther into the kitchen. If you stay where you are, it's only a matter of time before it finds you. But you can't run; it would spot you instantly. You look around frantically, trying to find a way out. The cabinet you just searched is almost empty; you could fit inside. But what if the Reagent starts looking inside them? Maybe you should crawl along the kitchen counters, try to make your way through the room to the doors. If you can get to the exit, you can make a run for it!

➤ **IF YOU WANT TO HIDE IN THE CABINET, TURN TO PAGE 104.**
➤ **IF YOU WANT TO CRAWL FOR THE EXIT, TURN TO PAGE 105.**

You're not sure what you hope to find, but you begin scouring the counters, looking around the various food machines, all shut down for the night. Working methodically, you go up and down the rows, but there's not much to be found. After a while, you begin to feel silly—especially given the events of the last two nights. You can't shake the feeling that this is another one of Gregory's games. It's a strange prank, to be sure, but maybe instead of trying to scare you, he wants your night tonight to be super . . . boring? Weird, for sure, but you wouldn't put it past him.

Suddenly, the door to the kitchen creaks open.

You turn, expecting Gregory and Freddy to be there, to tell you this was all another joke, but instead, there's an unfamiliar bot. It's unlike any of the other ones you've seen in the Pizzaplex; it's bigger, with ugly, insect-like eyes, and two "arms" that end in spray nozzles. On its back are several chemical tanks.

A cold feeling runs over your skin. Gregory wasn't joking.

And now the Reagent has spotted you. You try to run, but it's blocking the door. There's nowhere for you to go, and nothing to defend yourself with. You can only watch as it raises its arms and begins to spray some sort of gas into the air. It burns the moment it hits you, filling your nostrils, running down your throat, making your eyes water. You start to cough, but it doesn't help.

It's as if the Reagent has wrapped metallic hands around your throat and is choking you.

Desperate, you try to call for help. For Gregory, for Freddy, for anyone. But you can't breathe. The world starts to swirl, your vision going dark around the edges.

The last thing you see is the Reagent rolling forward, coming straight for you.

GAME OVER

➤ TO START FROM THE BEGINNING, TURN TO PAGE 3.
➤ TO TRY THIS NIGHT AGAIN, TURN TO PAGE 88.

There's no time to waste—the Reagent could spot you at any moment! You climb into the cabinet you just searched, pulling the door closed. In the dark, all you can hear is your heart pounding and the sound of the Reagent moving around the kitchen on its search. It must be going up and down the aisles; you hear it draw close, then move farther away. Then close again, then away.

Until suddenly, everything goes quiet.

You wait, ears straining. Minutes pass without any hint of where the Reagent is now. You're not sure what to do. Maybe the bot finished searching the kitchen and moved on. But you can't be sure of that. Fear grows, pressing on your chest like a heavy weight. If only this was one of Gregory's pranks. You'd welcome a joke—even a bad one—right now.

Inside the cabinet, everything remains as quiet as a grave. Maybe you should peek out and see if the bot is still there. Then again, if the Reagent hasn't left and you open the cabinet, it might see the movement. Staying put might be a better idea. But the longer you do that, the better the chance that the Reagent might decide to start searching the cabinets.

In the stifling dark, neither choice seems like a good one.

➤ **IF YOU WANT TO PEEK OUTSIDE AND SEE IF THE REAGENT IS GONE, TURN TO PAGE 106.**

➤ **IF YOU WANT TO STAY HIDDEN IN THE CABINET, TURN TO PAGE 107.**

You stay crouched down, peeking over the edge of the counter. The Reagent hasn't spotted you yet, and you're afraid that if you hide in a cabinet, the bot will start searching them and find you. You can't stay in the kitchen—you need to get out of here! If you crawl, keeping far away from the Reagent, you might be able to reach the kitchen doors and make a run for it, find Gregory and Freddy.

You move in the opposite direction of where the Reagent is, making your way down the aisle, checking around each turn as you inch closer to the door. You can hear the bot—somewhere—but crawling on the floor, the sound is distorted. You're a little surprised the bot can't hear your heart pounding in your chest.

Slowly, you travel around the edge of the kitchen, teeth gritted, expecting the Reagent to pop out at any moment. But by the time the kitchen doors are in sight, you've lost track of it altogether. Trying not to breathe too loud, you pause. The exit is only a dozen steps away.

Suddenly, you hear the whirr of movement. Down an aisle to one side of you, the Reagent appears. You duck back before it spots you, but now you're at the end of a row.

Trapped.

Maybe, if you're quick enough, you can make a run for the doors. But you're not sure. If you had a distraction, that *might* give you enough of a chance to get out the doors before the Reagent even knows you're there. But you're not sure about that, either.

The Reagent continues down the aisle, drawing closer.

You need to make a decision, and quick!

- **IF YOU HAVE A CAN OF SODARONI TO MAKE A DISTRACTION WITH, TURN TO PAGE 108.**
- **IF YOU WANT TO MAKE A RUN FOR IT, TURN TO PAGE 109.**

You can't hide in the cabinet forever. You listen again, hoping to hear movement, but everything is still silent. Taking a deep breath, you open the cabinet door a crack and try to spot the Reagent. You don't have much of a view, though. There's no movement, so if the bot is still around, it must not be looking where you are. You risk pushing the door out a little farther and slipping out, staying in a low crouch. Slowly, you peek over the edge of the counter.

The Reagent is standing on the other side.

Its head snaps down, eyes zeroing in on you.

A scream catches in your throat as the bot raises its arms and points at you. A moment later, gas begins hissing out of the nozzles, filling the air. A sickening, chemical smell overtakes you. You gag and duck back into the cabinet, pulling it shut. Your eyes and throat burn, and though you pull your shirt up over your nose, the air is already saturated with the Reagent's concoction. You decide to try to make a run for the exit, but the moment you move, vertigo seizes you, and you can't seem to make your arms move right. They're too heavy, as if made of lead. And even though the cabinet door is right in front of you, it might as well be on the other side of the Pizzaplex.

You're helpless.

Suddenly, the cabinet opens, light flooding in. A hand darts forward, grabbing you. Pulling you out. Lifting you.

You blink, eyes flooded with tears, and briefly, you see a face you recognize. A face you love.

Roxy.

Then, everything goes dark.

➤ TURN TO PAGE 118.

There's no way to tell if the Reagent is still in the kitchen, so to be on the safe side, you decide to stay hidden within the cabinet. You shift, trying not to make any noise as you wait. Minutes tick by. In the dark, with fear gripping you, it's hard to tell how many. The only thing you do know is that you really wish this was one of Gregory's jokes. You'd happily take a prank—even a mean one—at this point. Wherever Gregory and Freddy are now, you can only hope that they are working on a way to stop the Reagent.

If they can't, you may not make it until morning.

With every beat of your heart, you expect the door to fly open, for the Reagent to discover you. But there's nothing. No movement. No sounds.

Until a hiss begins.

At first, you don't understand what it is. Then the smell hits you—chemical and harsh, burning your nostrils and eyes. This must be the Reagent's fumes. It didn't find you, but it set its chemicals off anyway!

Smothered within seconds, you grab for the door. But it's like your body doesn't want to work; your limbs feel like they are a hundred pounds each. You start coughing. It's as if a hand is around your throat, squeezing.

A different kind of darkness comes over you, one that drags you down, swirling with vertigo. Somewhere in the distance, outside the cabinet, you think you hear a voice. A familiar voice.

Roxy?

Then, there's nothing.

GAME OVER

➤ TO START FROM THE BEGINNING, TURN TO PAGE 3.

➤ TO TRY THIS NIGHT AGAIN, TURN TO PAGE 88.

A distraction is what you need and, luckily, you've got just the thing to make it with!

You reach into your bag and pull out the can of Sodaroni, thankful you didn't get thirsty before this. You shake it up as hard as you can, then crack the tab and throw it in the opposite direction of the kitchen doors. It goes rolling along the floor, hissing and spitting out soda. Immediately, the Reagent reacts, surging forward after the unexpected new noise. As it goes for the can, you jump up and make a break for the door. You cover the distance easily, but as you try to push through the doors, they refuse to move.

The Reagent locked them!

Stifling a squeak of fear, you turn back to the bot, hoping it's still engaged with the can.

But no such luck.

The dark, insect-like eyes are trained on you. You glance around, desperate, and spot the fridge. Maybe if you can get to it, get inside and lock it before the Reagent catches you . . .

The moment you move the Reagent does, too. But the counters are between you and it, and it's hampered by them.

You can make it!

You're halfway to the fridge when the hissing starts. A noxious odor suddenly fills the air, burning your lungs, making you cough. You try to keep moving, but your step falters. The fridge, which seemed so close a moment ago, now looks miles away. You stumble, still gagging, and fall to your knees. Then to the floor.

You can't get up.

The edges of your vision blur and begin to turn dark. As the world begins to fade, a dark shape appears above you. At first, you think it's the Reagent.

Then you see purple lipstick and a streak of green hair.

The last thing you see before the darkness overtakes you is Roxy, reaching down for you.

➤ **REMOVE <u>CAN OF SODARONI</u> FROM YOUR INVENTORY AND TURN TO PAGE 118.**

You don't have a choice, you need to make a run for it before the Reagent reaches you. Taking a deep breath, you jump up and bolt for the door, feet pounding against the tile.

Immediately, you know you've been spotted. You hear the screech of wheels against floor tiles as the Reagent pursues you, but you've got a straight shot, and it still needs to navigate through the maze of counters. You can make it!

Then, you hear the hissing sound. You're almost to the door when the gas hits you, pervading the air around you, burning its way into your nostrils and down to your lungs. It burns your eyes, making them water. Still, you keep moving. The exit into the rest of the Pizzaplex is right in front of you, and if you can make it through the door, get into the fresh air, maybe you can find Gregory and Freddy. They'll be able to help—you just know it.

You take the last few steps to the doors, throwing yourself against them. But they don't budge. You try again, and again, but they refuse to open.

The Reagent locked them.

You turn, leaning into the locked exit to remain upright, blinking away tears. The Reagent is stopped a few steps away, gas still streaming from its nozzles, just watching.

Waiting.

It doesn't have to wait long.

GAME OVER

➤ TO START FROM THE BEGINNING, TURN TO PAGE 3.
➤ TO TRY THIS NIGHT AGAIN, TURN TO PAGE 88.

You remember the food service key card you found and take it out of your bag, hoping it will work. One swipe later and the keypad lights up green. *Success!*

You push the door open and head out into the hallway, hoping that it's not too late to catch up with Gregory and Freddy. If this is a joke, they're probably headed to play video games in one of the arcades while laughing about you being stuck in the kitchen.

You turn a corner when suddenly, a little way ahead, a bot appears. But it's unlike any bot you've ever seen before in the Pizzaplex. It's larger, with two "arms" that end in nozzles, tanks on its back, and a blank, scary face dominated by dark, buggy eyes. You duck back into the hall, heart pounding. It must be the Reagent that Gregory was talking about.

He wasn't lying!

Terrified, you retreat back into the kitchen and shut the door. The faint sound of the bot approaching gradually grows louder. You look around, searching for a good place to hide. You don't have much time to decide. There are a lot of cabinets, some of which are large enough to hold you. There's also a freezer door on the other side of the kitchen. Maybe the Reagent wouldn't think to look for anyone in there?

➤ IF YOU WANT TO HIDE IN A CABINET, TURN TO PAGE 111.

➤ IF YOU WANT TO HIDE IN THE FREEZER, TURN TO PAGE 112.

You need to be quick, so you decide to hide in one of the nearby cabinets. You run over, throwing open the doors until you find one empty enough for you to fit inside. Getting in, you shut the door moments before you hear the kitchen doors open. The Reagent rolls into the room. You can't see it, but you can hear it moving around, searching, looking for any organic matter to "neutralize." You clench your fists, hoping that it only does a perfunctory sweep of the kitchen and doesn't think to start searching the cabinets.

It's dark in your cabinet, and your breathing feels very loud. You try to take each breath as silently as possible as your ears strain for whatever is happening outside your hiding spot. The sounds of the Reagent continue but become fewer and farther between. Then, after a few minutes, it's silent.

You wait, afraid to move in case the bot is still nearby. But if it *is* gone, maybe you can take the chance to run, and find Gregory and Freddy again. They said they were going to try to stop the Reagent. No matter what they think, you'd feel safer with them, helping them do whatever they have planned. Then again, you have no idea if the Reagent has left the kitchen. If it's still around, you don't want to risk revealing yourself.

➤ IF YOU WANT TO PEEK OUT AND SEE IF THE REAGENT IS GONE, TURN TO PAGE 113.

➤ IF YOU WANT TO REMAIN HIDDEN, TURN TO PAGE 114.

If there's anywhere the Reagent won't think to look, it's in the freezer. You rush over to it, pulling the door open and slipping inside right as a shadow crosses the kitchen door window. A moment after you shut yourself inside, those doors open and the Reagent rolls in.

You cross your arms, hugging yourself. It's cold inside the freezer, frost lining the walls and little icicles hanging from the shelves. Your only company is the many boxes of frozen foods and, more exciting, tub after tub of ice cream. On another night, you might have been able to have fun in here, trying all the flavors from Chica's Chocolate to Roxy's Rocky Road. Gregory would definitely like it. You wonder where he and Freddy are, and if they've managed to do anything that might stop the Reagent. Whatever they are working on, you hope they figure it out fast!

It's hard to hear outside the freezer, but if you press your ear to the frosty door, you can just make out the sounds of the Reagent moving around the kitchen, searching. Minutes tick by. The noises grow softer and more intermittent, and then fade away entirely. Does that mean the Reagent is gone? Or are your ears just starting to freeze? Teeth chattering, you consider your options. You could risk looking outside to see if the bot has finished its sweep of the kitchen and moved on to somewhere else. But what if it is still out there? You look around the freezer again. If the Reagent *is* still out there, maybe there's something you can use as a distraction, and then make a break for it?

- **IF YOU WANT TO PEEK OUT AND SEE IF THE REAGENT IS GONE, TURN TO PAGE 115.**
- **IF YOU WANT TO FIND SOMETHING IN THE FREEZER TO USE AS A DISTRACTION, TURN TO PAGE 116.**

The silence continues. Eventually, you can't stand it, and decide you have to see if the Reagent is still in the kitchen. Slowly, you crack the door to the cabinet and look out. In the dim lighting, you can't see much, just the empty aisle of the kitchen, with no bot in sight. You open it a little wider and stick your head out to look around. One side of the aisle is still clear, all the way to the end. The other . . .

When you look the opposite way, the Reagent is right there—almost close enough to touch!

In a panic, you pull back into the cabinet, slamming the door shut and holding it. There's no way you're stronger than the bot, but you don't know what else to do. Weirdly enough, it doesn't try to get at you. At first, you don't understand why . . . and then you hear the hissing.

Suddenly, a sharp, chemical smell fills the air within the cabinet. You begin to cough, your eyes and throat burning. It's unbearable. You open the door, trying to flee, but it's even worse outside. The Reagent is nearly on top of you spraying its noxious gases. It doesn't try to attack, though, so you stumble away, trying to reach the kitchen door. The room starts to spin. Before you know it, you've fallen, landing on your back. The last thing you see is the Reagent looming above you, still spraying.

Then, nothing.

GAME OVER

> TO START FROM THE BEGINNING, TURN TO PAGE 3.

> TO TRY THIS NIGHT AGAIN, TURN TO PAGE 88.

Without knowing for sure whether the Reagent is gone, you're too afraid to risk leaving the cabinet. Instead, you stay balled up in the dark space, heart pounding in your ears as you listen for any clues as to where the bot might be. Or for Gregory and Freddy. Wherever they are, you really hope they are working on finding a way to disable the Reagent, and that they are doing it quickly! If only you'd been able to catch up with them before the Reagent appeared. Maybe you would have been able to do something to help.

More time ticks by in the dark silence. Sometimes, you think you hear something, but the noises are so faint you aren't sure if it's the Reagent or your fear playing tricks on you. Which is why you aren't sure you hear the hissing . . . until it keeps going and the smell hits you.

Noxious, burning . . . Whatever fills the air immediately begins to burn your eyes and throat. You try to stifle a cough, but after a few more seconds it's impossible to contain. You can barely breathe!

There's no choice now; the Reagent must have heard you, which means you need to make a run for it! But as you reach for the cabinet door, your head swims, and your arms start feeling like they weigh a hundred pounds. Still, you fight to lift them, to get out of there . . .

It's too late. The door to the cabinet flies open, the light causing you to blink. Your heart sinks. The Reagent has found you.

But the face that appears isn't the bot. You see purple makeup, a streak of green hair . . .

Roxy!

The last thing you see is Roxanne Wolf reaching for you. Then the world goes dark.

➤ **TURN TO PAGE 118.**

You wait and listen, hoping to get some hint of whether the Reagent is still in the kitchen, but the longer you wait, the colder the room is getting. Your nose is already running and your fingers are beginning to feel numb. You can't stay in the freezer all night. If you do, Gregory is going to find you in the morning as frozen as one of the Popsicles!

You creep over to the door and pull the latch, opening it a few inches. Beyond it, the kitchen is full of shadows, but even though you wait, you don't see or hear anything moving. Heart pounding, you open it a little more until you can see the kitchen doors. They're just across the room, the light beyond them beckoning with what feels like relative safety. All you want to do right now is get out of here, find Gregory and Freddy, and figure out a way to shut down the Reagent!

There's no point in waiting any longer. You step outside the kitchen, ready to run for the door.

Suddenly, there's movement out of the corner of your eye. You turn and come face-to-face with the Reagent. It's so close that you jump back, right as it lifts its arms to release a stream of noxious gas. The gas hits like a flame, immediately burning your eyes and making its way down your throat, into your lungs. You gasp and try to run, coughing so hard it hurts. But as you move, your limbs seem to get heavier and heavier until you're barely stumbling. The kitchen doors, which looked close only a moment before, now look as if they are miles away.

Still, you push yourself to reach them and the fresh air beyond. The room swims. You fall, your vision growing dark around the edges.

The last thing you see is the Reagent rolling closer before it all goes dark.

GAME OVER

➤ TO START FROM THE BEGINNING, TURN TO PAGE 3.
➤ TO TRY THIS NIGHT AGAIN, TURN TO PAGE 88.

If you're going to risk going out into the kitchen without knowing whether the Reagent has finished its search and moved on, you should try to find something to use as a distraction. You search around, combing through the frozen food boxes on the shelves. But after a few minutes, you begin to get discouraged. You're not sure what kind of distraction you can make using jalapeño poppers and fish sticks. Maybe the Reagent is a fan of ice cream? You give up, pretty sure a Minty Gator cone isn't going to get you out of this situation.

As you turn away, trying to come up with another idea, your elbow hits a box sitting on the edge of a shelf. It goes flying, spilling frozen corn dogs that clatter across the floor. Your heart jumps into your throat; beyond the freezer door, something is moving—and fast! You rush over, holding the latch shut right as the Reagent tries to open it. It takes all your strength, but you manage to keep it closed, and after a few more tugs, the bot gives up. Still holding the door, you take a deep breath, relieved.

Then, the hissing begins.

However, you don't realize what you're hearing until the gas begins to creep around the edges of the door. It hits you like a punch to the face, noxious and burning, making your eyes water. Unable to stop yourself, you let go of the handle, pulling your shirt up over your mouth and nose. But it barely helps. The gas keeps coming, filling the freezer.

Your head starts to swim and your knees go weak; you crumple to the floor, among the strewn corn dogs that gave you away. *Such a ridiculous way to go*, you think, as your vision begins to go fuzzy around the edges. *Death by corn dog.*

Suddenly, the door of the freezer flies open. You blink, resigned that the Reagent has found you and cornered you, as a blurry figure steps into view. There's nowhere to run.

But it's not the bot. A face you know—a face you adore—stares down at you, full of concern.

The last thing you see is Roxy, reaching for you.
Then it goes dark.

➤ **TURN TO PAGE 118.**

NIGHT 4

"Hmmm."

"Cassie, wake up!"

You open your eyes. Fear sends you bolting upright, thinking the Reagent is still nearby, but once you blink the sleep from your eyes, you realize what you are seeing is purple and green light, not the darkness of the kitchen. You're in Roxy's greenroom. And standing above you, staring down with concern, is Roxy.

"What—?" Your mouth is as dry as sand, making it hard to talk, but Roxy hands you a can of Fizzy Faz. You sip it slowly, washing away the lingering taste of the Reagent's chemicals. Your throat still burns a little, but the drink helps.

"Thank goodness you finally woke up," Roxy says.

Confused, you blink at her. But also, you're happy and relieved to see Roxy. You can't help but feel safe around her. "What happened?"

"I rescued you from the Reagent." Roxy steps away, wringing her hands. "You inhaled some of the chemicals, but I got to you soon enough. Still, you've been asleep all day."

So it's night again. You swallow the last of the soda, trying to process what's happened. "Where are Gregory and Freddy?" Did they even care that the Reagent almost got you? Or did the Reagent get to Gregory first?

Roxy shrugs. "I don't know, Cassie. I only found you."

"What about the Reagent?"

You don't like how Roxy glances around uneasily. "It deactivated for the day, but now that it's night again, it's going to continue with its programming until all the organic matter in the Pizzaplex is . . ." She pauses. "Dealt with."

After what happened last night, the last thing you want is to be "dealt with." If only Freddy had let you leave the other night, you wouldn't be in this mess! And what happened to Gregory? If Roxy hasn't seen him, he might be in trouble. But there's no way you can search the Pizzaplex for him with the Reagent active. Wherever Gregory is, he's unfortunately on his own!

"Roxy," you say, "I need to leave the Pizzaplex. Will you help me find a way out?"

Roxy thinks for a moment, then nods. "It's too dangerous for you to be here right now, Cassie. If there's a way to get out, we'll find it."

"All right." You know the Reagent is out there, but you're not as scared as you were last night. Not with Roxy helping you. With her, it feels like you have a chance. But that doesn't mean you don't need to be careful. With the threat of danger still lurking around the Pizzaplex, you're going to have to be smart in order to escape, and not give the Reagent a chance to corner you! "Let's go!"

With Roxy on your heels, you start for the door. It would be a good idea to move slowly, making sure to search as you go. Then again, maybe it would be better to figure out exactly where the Reagent is, so you can avoid it. There are monitors in the backstage office. If you check there, you might be able to see where the bot is.

You glance back at Roxy, who gives you an encouraging smile. You smile back, but even with her backing you up, you're starting to feel vulnerable again. The Reagent is really dangerous, and you'd feel better about traversing the Pizzaplex if you had some defense. Except . . . you're not sure where to look for something like that. The crate you saw earlier in Monty's greenroom occurs to you. Maybe you should check that out again and see if it has anything that can help you?

No matter what, you've had enough of the Pizzaplex. It's time to find a way out!

- IF YOU HAVE THE EXECUTIVE CLEARANCE KEY CARD AND WANT TO CHECK THE CRATE IN MONTY'S GREENROOM, TURN TO PAGE 121.
- IF YOU WANT TO SEARCH THE HALLWAY CAREFULLY BEFORE PROCEEDING, TURN TO PAGE 122.
- IF YOU WANT TO HEAD FOR THE BACKSTAGE OFFICE TO CHECK THE MONITORS, TURN TO PAGE 123.

You wonder if the Executive Clearance key card would make a difference in opening the crate you saw in Monty's greenroom.

"Roxy, we need to make a stop."

Roxy supportively follows as you creep down the hallway into the next greenroom. Monty is absent, thankfully. You're not sure if Gregory was telling the truth about fixing his programming or not, but you'd rather not have to deal with Monty right now.

You go over to the crate and inspect the lock again. Taking out the Executive Clearance key card, you slip it into the card reader. A moment later, it flashes green. You hear a click as the box unlocks.

"Success!" you announce.

"Oooh." Roxy leans closer. "What's inside?"

"I'm not sure, but let's find out!" You raise the top of the crate.

Inside, there are a pair of arms. Arms for Monty, you realize—brand-new and tipped with flashy, silver metal claws. They're heavy, but you manage to pull one out and inspect the connections. Then, you smile.

"Hey, Roxy. How do you feel about getting an upgrade?"

A little while later, Roxy shows off her brand-new arms, the silver metal flashing in the neon lights.

Roxy grins. "Oh, forget Monty. These look great on *me*."

"They do," you heartily agree. "Now let's find a way out of here!"

With Roxy equipped with the new claws, your apprehension settles a bit, and you feel far more prepared for whatever the Pizzaplex plans to throw at you tonight.

- **ADD MONTY'S CLAWS TO ROXY AND TURN TO PAGE 118.**
- **ADD MONTY'S CLAWS TO ROXY. IF YOU WANT TO SEARCH THE HALLWAY CAREFULLY BEFORE PROCEEDING, TURN TO PAGE 122.**
- **ADD MONTY'S CLAWS TO ROXY. IF YOU WANT TO HEAD FOR THE BACKSTAGE OFFICE TO CHECK THE MONITORS, TURN TO PAGE 123.**

Peeking out of Roxy's greenroom, you look carefully down the hall in both directions. So far, so good. The Reagent isn't right outside the greenrooms, but for all you know it could be around any corner. You take a few steps out, heading down the hallway. Roxy follows you, staying close as you make your way toward the mainstage area. But once you are there, you hesitate, unsure what the best way out of the Pizzaplex will be.

"I need to find the closest exit," you say quietly, mulling your options over.

"The fastest way would be out the front entrance," Roxy says. "We should head that way."

She's right. But that's also right in the main lobby, so if the Reagent is anywhere nearby, it might see or hear you. It's not a *bad* idea, but you're not sure if it's the smartest one. You wish you knew exactly where the Reagent was right now.

"I don't know," you say. "Maybe we should head for a less obvious exit, like the Loading Dock."

Roxy puts a hand on your shoulder. "It's up to you, Cassie. Whichever way you want to go, I'll go with you and help as much as I can."

You smile. Roxy's promise makes you feel safer than you probably are. At the same time, you're not sure which way would give you the best chance of eluding the Reagent.

➤ **IF YOU WANT TO SEARCH THE MAIN ENTRANCE, TURN TO PAGE 144.**

➤ **IF YOU WANT TO HEAD FOR THE LOADING DOCK, TURN TO PAGE 145.**

You'd definitely feel more comfortable if you knew exactly where the Reagent was.

"C'mon, Roxy." You lead her down the hall. "Let's go to the backstage office and see if we can find anything on the monitors."

"Good idea," Roxy agrees, which makes you feel like this is the right decision. In fact, having Roxy with you makes you feel much better in general. Maybe someday Roxy will be as good a friend to you as Freddy is to Gregory.

Carefully, you make your way to the backstage office and try the door, but it's locked! You try again, confused since you and Gregory have snuck inside plenty of times; but maybe with the Reagent active, security levels are higher in the Pizzaplex.

"Roxy, can you open it?"

The animatronic shakes her head. "Sorry, Cassie, but I don't have access. You need a backstage office key card to open that door right now."

- **IF YOU HAVE THE EXECUTIVE CLEARANCE KEY CARD AND WANT TO OPEN THE DOOR, TURN TO PAGE 124.**
- **IF YOU DON'T HAVE A KEY CARD, GO BACK TO PAGE 118.**
- **IF YOU WANT TO SEARCH THE HALLWAY CAREFULLY BEFORE PROCEEDING, TURN TO PAGE 122.**

Your hopes dip a little at what Roxy says, but then you remember the card you found. It would open the backstage office, wouldn't it? You pull it from your bag and swipe it through the lock. With a bright beep, the lock disengages, and the door opens.

Success!

Inside, you immediately head for the monitors lining the wall. You can see almost every corner of the Pizzaplex from here. With any luck, the Reagent will be in one of those corners.

"There it is!" Roxy points.

You look at the monitor she's indicating, which shows the inside of the Superstar Daycare. There, the Reagent is making a slow search, occasionally pausing to spray chemicals here and there. You spent a lot of time in the daycare when you were younger, with a lot of kids who tended to eat too many sweets and slices of pizza, so you are sure there is plenty of leftover "organic material" for the Reagent to clean. If you're lucky, maybe it will be occupied there for most of the night!

Movement on another monitor catches your eye—this time something far more exciting. It's Gregory and Freddy! They're tiny figures on the screen, so you can't quite make out what they are doing, but you can see that they are in the Prize Counter. And right out in the open!

"We need to warn Gregory," you say.

Roxy nods. "Yes, Freddy may not be able to protect him."

The Reagent is distracted for now, though, so maybe you should take this opportunity to search the backstage office and see if there's anything that can help you against the Reagent.

➤ **IF YOU SEARCH THE BACKSTAGE OFFICE, TURN TO PAGE 125.**

➤ **IF YOU WANT TO GO IMMEDIATELY WARN GREGORY, TURN TO PAGE 126.**

The Reagent seems engaged enough, so you decide to risk looking around the office.

"Roxy," you say, "Can you see if there's anything we can use against the Reagent in here? There must be a way to stop it somehow!"

Roxy heads for the opposite end of the room as you start searching, opening the few drawers and cabinets you see. There aren't many, and most are filled with things like pens and other office supplies. Nothing that's going to do you much good against a bot who can melt you in a matter of minutes! Just remembering the chemicals makes your throat tighten up again. You're sure to check the monitors every so often as you search, making sure both the Reagent and Gregory and Freddy are still in sight.

"Cassie," Roxy calls. "Come look at this."

You go over to where she is standing, next to one of the control panels. Inserted in one of them is a metal key. You're not sure what it is, but it looks like it could be important. *And* like it might work in more places than just the backstage office.

"Should I take it?"

Roxy shrugs. "I don't know what it's a key for."

You're not sure if you should take it, especially if Roxy doesn't know its purpose. But for all you know, it might help you open an exit door in the Pizzaplex, and help you escape the Reagent before it has a chance to corner you again!

➤ **IF YOU DECIDE TO LEAVE THE KEY BEHIND, TURN TO PAGE 128.**

➤ **IF YOU WANT TO TAKE THE KEY, TURN TO PAGE 129.**

There's no time to waste—you need to warn Gregory about the Reagent before it finds him and Freddy! You keep quiet as you and Roxy leave the backstage office behind, moving as fast as you can while still keeping an eye out for the bot. It may be distracted in the daycare for now, but there's no knowing how long that might last. At any moment, it may decide to move on to another part of the Pizzaplex, and if that happens, both you and Gregory will be in danger!

Fortunately, decontaminating the Superstar Daycare seems to keep the Reagent busy as you don't encounter it, or any other bot, on your way back into the main lobby area of the Pizzaplex. You're also relieved to see that Gregory and Freddy are still where you saw them on the monitors, in the Prize Counter, surrounded by all sorts of Freddy Fazbear collectibles and merchandise.

You're about to call out to Gregory when you notice something strange. Gregory and Freddy seem to be arguing, and Freddy is beginning to look . . . angry? You're not close enough to make out what they are saying, but as soon as you begin to move closer, Freddy suddenly lets out an angry growl. He grabs Gregory, who looks shocked, and lifts him from the ground.

"Cassie, don't look!" Roxy grabs you and pulls you to her so that you don't see what happens next. But she doesn't cover your ears, so you still hear Gregory's terrified scream.

Your blood runs cold as you push away from Roxy. You have to see. But when you manage to look back, Gregory is limp in Freddy's arms.

You let out a little noise. Gregory is dead!

There's no time for you to figure out what has happened. Alerted by the sound you made, Freddy's head snaps in your direction. He growls again and begins to run, coming straight for you!

"Run, Cassie!" Roxy cries.

You're moving before she finishes the words, retreating. You need to get somewhere safe, and fast. But where should you run? If you can get back to Roxy's greenroom, you can lock the door. More than anything right now, you want to get out of the Pizzaplex. Maybe you should run for the front entrance?

- **IF YOU WANT TO MAKE A RUN FOR ROXY'S GREENROOM, TURN TO PAGE 141.**
- **IF YOU WANT TO RUN FOR THE FRONT ENTRANCE, TURN TO PAGE 143.**

You examine the metal key—and the console that it's inserted in—for a few more seconds. But there's something about it you don't like. It's one thing to retrieve a lost key card and use it, but this key is still in the control panel. For all you know, it's making sure something important happens . . . or *doesn't* happen. You decide to leave it behind for another time.

You wave Roxy away from the console and finish your search of the backstage office. To your dismay, there's nothing that's going to help you against the Reagent, and you've wasted enough time as it is. You take one last glance at the monitors to confirm everyone is where they were a few minutes ago.

"Okay," you say to Roxy. "Let's go warn Gregory about the Reagent before it's too late!"

➤ **TURN TO PAGE 126.**

The metal key looks too important not to take with you. You reach for it.

"Cassie, are you sure that's a good idea?" Roxy asks.

You hesitate, but with the Reagent active, you need every advantage you can get. Your fingers take hold of the key. You have to fiddle with it a little, but after a moment, it comes free.

Suddenly, an alarm sounds.

Lights flash across the console as you jump back, dropping the key. It clatters away under the console, out of reach.

"Oh no . . ." says Roxy.

Oh no is right. You get down on your hands and knees, trying to retrieve the key, to put it back and maybe stop the alarm, but the opening under the console is too narrow. You can't reach it. You jump up instead, searching the console for a way to turn the alarm off.

"Roxy, can you help?"

The animatronic starts pressing buttons and flipping switches, but to no avail. The alarm wails in your ears. You stop and take a deep breath, forcing yourself to look at the console calmly. You press a few more buttons, type in some commands.

Finally, the klaxon stops.

You exhale in relief, your ears still ringing. But when you look back at the monitors, your stomach drops.

The Reagent is no longer in the daycare.

Roxy sees this, too. "I think we need to get out of here."

"Good idea." You go over to the door and look out into the hall. There's nothing out there . . . yet. You can take a left or a right, but without knowing where the Reagent is, you can only guess which way is safe. You hesitate, wondering whether you might be better off closing the door to the backstage office and locking it.

- **IF YOU WANT TO LOCK THE DOOR, TURN TO PAGE 131.**
- **IF YOU WANT TO LEAVE THE OFFICE AND TAKE A LEFT DOWN THE HALLWAY, TURN TO PAGE 132.**
- **IF YOU WANT TO LEAVE THE OFFICE AND TAKE A RIGHT DOWN THE HALLWAY, TURN TO PAGE 134.**

You hesitate to leave the backstage office without knowing where the Reagent might be now. For all you know, the moment you head into the hall it will appear. You shut the door instead. Thankfully, you can use the backstage office key card to lock it again. The display inside flashes red, and you take a step back.

"Cassie, look!" Roxy exclaims.

You turn back toward her and the monitors. The Reagent is in sight again. In fact, it's very nearly at the backstage office! You watch on the cameras as it rolls closer, finally coming to a stop outside the office door. It examines the entrance as if confused about what to do next.

Then, suddenly, it raises one of its arms and touches the end to the keypad.

Inside, the keypad you just locked flashes green.

"Look out!" Roxy calls as the door swings open. You try to grab the door to slam it shut, but it's too late. The Reagent rolls forward, blocking you from closing it.

And the minute it spots you . . .

Gas fills the air again. You try to turn away but it overwhelms you within moments. The last thing you see is Roxy coming for you, reaching out.

Then, nothing.

GAME OVER

> TO START FROM THE BEGINNING, TURN TO PAGE 3.
> TO TRY THIS NIGHT AGAIN, TURN TO PAGE 118.

Being decisive, you take a left down the hallway, leaving the backstage office behind. Roxy stays close to you as you move as quickly as you dare, as quietly as a mouse. You expect the Reagent to appear at any moment, corner you, and start spraying its horrible chemicals again. Luckily, it remains engaged as you make it back into the atrium area of the Pizzaplex, and head to where you saw Gregory and Freddy on the monitor.

Normally, you love the Prize Counter. It's filled with all sorts of cool Freddy Fazbear and Glamrock Band–themed items. Obviously, Roxy is your favorite member of the band, and you like to collect her merch, but having the real deal with you is even better. Seeing you glancing back at her, Roxy gives you a thumbs-up, which leaves a warm feeling in your chest.

Finally, you get close enough to see the Prize Counter. To your relief, Gregory and Freddy are still there. But your step slows as you realize that something seems off. Freddy is looming over Gregory, and they seem to be arguing, but you can't hear what they are saying.

"Roxy, what's going on?"

Your animatronic friend comes to a stop beside you. "I'm not sure, Cassie. But Freddy looks *mad*."

Before you have a chance to say anything else, Freddy suddenly lets out a roar and raises his claws. Then, he reaches for Gregory—

"Cassie, don't look!" Roxy pulls you away, turning you so your face is pressed into her side. Behind you, Gregory lets out a bloodcurdling scream. When Roxy's grip finally loosens and you are able to turn back, Freddy is holding Gregory, who is limp.

Dead.

A scream gets stuck in your throat as you go cold all over. *Freddy . . . killed . . .* You shake your head, unable to understand.

Suddenly, Freddy's head snaps up, turning in your direction. He snarls again and begins running straight for you.

"Run, Cassie!"

You don't need Roxy's instruction to start doing that. Whatever is happening with Freddy, he's coming after you next. You have to get away! Still wary of the Reagent, you think of Roxy's greenroom. Maybe that space will be safe. But another part of you wants to risk passing near the daycare and making a break for the front doors instead.

- **IF YOU WANT TO MAKE A RUN FOR ROXY'S GREENROOM, TURN TO PAGE 137.**
- **IF YOU WANT TO RUN FOR THE FRONT DOORS, TURN TO PAGE 139.**

One direction seems as good as the other, so you opt to take a right out of the backstage office. You move as quickly as you dare, but quietly, making your way down the hallway with Roxy only a couple of steps behind. You thought you felt safer with the animatronic by your side, but the Reagent seems relentless in its mission. And after setting off that alarm, you bet it knows exactly where to find you. The only thing you can do is *not* be in that place when it gets there!

You're almost to the mainstage area when, suddenly, you see movement. It's the Reagent, coming your way! You throw a hand up to stop Roxy and freeze, unsure of what to do next. You can try to make a run for it, heading in the opposite direction. Other than that . . .

Roxy taps on your shoulder. You look back and find her pointing to the band's Rehearsal Room, which isn't far away. If you head for that, you might be able to avoid the Reagent as well.

The Reagent is getting closer with every second that ticks by. You need to decide which way to go, and quickly!

> **IF YOU WANT TO MAKE A RUN FOR IT, TURN TO PAGE 135.**
> **IF YOU WANT TO HIDE IN THE REHEARSAL ROOM, TURN TO PAGE 136.**

There's no time to waste. You turn, grabbing Roxy.

"Run!" you whisper.

It takes a moment for the animatronic to react, but then she's running with you, back in the direction you came from. At first, you think you've gotten away in time.

Then you hear: "Cassie, it's coming!"

Roxy's cry turns your blood to ice water. You can't help it; you risk a glance back. The Reagent has spotted you and is pursuing, moving faster than you expected the bot to be able to. You hear the hissing noise again.

Within moments, the bot has nearly caught up to you, its terrible arms raised, spewing noxious gas. Those insectile eyes are locked on you, narrowed with purpose. You try to hold your breath, to not breathe in the gases, but it's impossible. Like last time, they burn and choke. You stumble. Roxy keeps moving, not seeing you falter.

"Roxy!" you gasp.

When she hears your voice, she stops and turns around. But you know it's already too late.

You stumble again, falling to your knees as the world goes dark.

GAME OVER

➤ TO START FROM THE BEGINNING, TURN TO PAGE 3.

➤ TO TRY THIS NIGHT AGAIN, TURN TO PAGE 118.

Right before the Reagent gets close enough to spot you, you grab Roxy by the arm and drag her into the Rehearsal Room. You close the door, hoping the Reagent doesn't see the movement, then press yourselves to either side of it. It's dark in the Rehearsal Room, with all the lights turned off since it's not in use, but you can see the skeletal outlines of instruments and equipment by the thin line of light that shines through the narrow window in the door.

You can only hope the Reagent won't decide to glance inside.

From where you are, you can't see the bot, but you can hear it rolling closer. Across from you, Roxy raises one finger to her lips: *Be quiet*. The bot must be right outside the door. And then: A shadow falls across the window, making it even darker. For a moment, you're sure that the Reagent has trapped you, that it's about to open the door and release its awful chemicals into the room. But after a long minute, it continues to roll on toward the backstage office.

You let out a sigh of relief.

Roxy does the same. "That was close."

"Too close," you agree. But now that the Reagent is gone, you need to go find Gregory and warn him. "C'mon, we have to get to the Prize Counter before it's too late!"

➤ TURN TO PAGE 140.

Terrified, you bolt in the direction of the greenrooms again, Roxy staying close beside you.

Tears fill your eyes. You wipe at them. Poor Gregory. "What's wrong with Freddy?"

"I don't know," says Roxy. "Something must have messed with his programming."

It doesn't make sense, but there's no time to figure it out now. You can hear Freddy behind you, gaining on you as you run across the Pizzaplex to the stage area. It feels like a hundred miles; you can't seem to move fast enough. Finally, you turn down the hallway, then into Roxy's greenroom.

"Close the door!"

Roxy obeys, but as she shuts the door, you can tell something is wrong. Roxy taps at the door. "It won't lock!"

You push forward, giving it a try. The keypad should allow you to lock the door, but no matter what you try, it remains unsecured. Frustration and fear grip you. You need more time to figure this out, more time to—

The door bursts open, sending you stumbling backward. Freddy, even more enraged than the other night, stomps forward.

"Freddy, stop!" Roxy cries, and protectively steps in front of you.

But Freddy just shoves her to one side as if she's a doll. Then there's nothing left between you and him, and he's bearing down on you, claws raised . . .

You close your eyes and scream.

But nothing happens.

Reluctantly, you open one eye. Freddy is standing a few steps away now. His chest opens to reveal Gregory, very much alive. He jumps down, laughing. Freddy joins in.

And worst of all, so does Roxy.

"Got you again!" Gregory cries, with a grin that makes you feel like something sharp is stabbing into your stomach.

Your mouth drops open. "Another prank? That wasn't funny, Gregory!"

"It *was* a little funny." Roxy comes over and tries to help you up, but you shake her off.

"You were in on it, too?"

Roxy nods. "Gregory said you like being scared. That it would be fun. Didn't you have fun, Cassie?"

"No!" you cry. You want to say more, to rip into Gregory and his horrible sense of humor. But cornered by him and Freddy—and now, Roxy—the words stick to your tongue. Instead, you glare at Gregory one last time and run off.

➤ **TURN TO PAGE 168.**

Gregory is dead. The Reagent is still out there. There's no question about it now, you need to get out of the Pizzaplex as fast as you can! You run for the front doors, through the upstairs lobby area and down the stairs. Roxy keeps pace with you, but you can also hear Freddy in pursuit, growing closer.

At the bottom of the stairs, Roxy pauses.

"You keep running," she says. "Maybe I can reason with Freddy."

"Roxy, no!"

"Go, Cassie!" Roxy orders.

You don't want to keep going, but you do, running across the smooth tile to where the main entrance of the Pizzaplex is. That's where you need to get to, and it's the only thing you can focus on; the doors grow larger in your vision until, after what feels like an eternity, you reach them. You're too afraid to look back, not wanting to see what befell Gregory happen to Roxy, too. Instead, you try to open the door.

But it won't budge.

You push again, shaking it as hard as you can, but it refuses to let you out. You try another, and another. But they all remain stubbornly closed.

There's a sound behind you.

Slowly, you turn. But it's not Roxy, or even Freddy, that's joined you at the doors.

It's the Reagent.

You try to cry out for Roxy, but before you can open your mouth, the Reagent's arms fly up and its gases begin to spray. Your scream turns into coughing . . . then choking. Falling back against the locked doors, you slide to the floor as the world starts to gets fuzzy.

Slowly, it goes dark.

GAME OVER

➤ TO START FROM THE BEGINNING, TURN TO PAGE 3.

➤ TO TRY THIS NIGHT AGAIN, TURN TO PAGE 118.

With the Reagent heading in the opposite direction, you take the opportunity to run for the Prize Counter. You're relieved to see Gregory and Freddy are still there. But as you get closer, you realize something is wrong. Gregory and Freddy seem to be arguing, though you can't hear what they are saying. The one thing you can tell is that Freddy looks *mad*. You start to call out, to warn Gregory about the Reagent, but before you're able to, Freddy suddenly lets out a roar. He raises his claws and reaches for Gregory—

"Cassie, don't look!" Roxy grabs you, spinning you so that you don't see what comes next. Still, you hear Gregory's scream, a sound that makes you feel cold all over. You don't want to look, but you have to—pulling away from Roxy, you turn back.

Freddy is holding Gregory's limp body.

Dead.

You can't believe it. Why would Freddy turn on Gregory like that? You're trying to make sense of it when Freddy's head snaps up. With a snarl, he bolts toward you.

"Run, Cassie!" Roxy cries.

You obey, terrified. You have no idea why, but Freddy has gone wild, and he's coming for you next! You have to get somewhere safe! Roxy's greenroom isn't far; you can lock the door. Or maybe you should risk passing the Reagent and run for the front entrance instead. Freddy can't follow you if you get out of the Pizzaplex!

- **IF YOU WANT TO MAKE A RUN FOR ROXY'S GREENROOM, TURN TO PAGE 137.**
- **IF YOU WANT TO RUN FOR THE FRONT DOORS, TURN TO PAGE 139.**

Almost too scared to think, you bolt back in the direction of the greenrooms. Roxy is on your heels, but you can hear Freddy behind her, getting closer with every passing second. He's snarling and making weird noises. Is this what happened to Monty? Was Gregory playing around with his programming, too, and maybe messed something up?

There's no way to know. Not now, when Gregory is . . .

You can't think about it. Focusing on running, you make it back to the stage area and into Roxy's greenroom. She follows you in and shuts the door, locking it. And not a moment too soon. The whole room seems to shudder as Freddy collides with the exterior of the door. You scream, unable to stop yourself, and retreat back from the door.

"What's wrong with Freddy?!" You shudder as Gregory's scream echoes in your ears. "Why did he do that?"

"I don't know." Roxy winces as Freddy collides with the door again.

"LET ME IN!" Freddy roars.

The next time Freddy hits the door, it begins to splinter around the edges.

Your heart drops. There's not much time before Freddy breaks through! You look around, but there's nowhere to go, only . . .

You spot a vent up in one corner of the room.

"Roxy," you cry out, pointing, "help me up there!"

Understanding, Roxy goes over to the vent and rips the cover off. Freddy slams into the door again, the cracks growing larger.

"Hurry!"

Roxy hoists you up. You grab the edges of the opening, trying to pull yourself up. Behind you, the door explodes inward and Freddy bursts in, growling as he lunges for you. He shoves Roxy aside and you fall to the floor.

Suddenly, above you, there's nothing but teeth.

You throw your hands over your eyes and scream.

But . . . nothing happens. Laughter slowly fills the room. When you look up again, Freddy's chest is open, and Gregory is crouched in there, alive. And laughing his head off. Freddy has joined in, and anger surges through you as you realize they've pulled another prank. But then, you look at Roxy and your heart drops.

She's laughing, too.

Your anger fizzles, dampened by embarrassment and a rising feeling of betrayal.

"This was all a *joke*?" you say, hardly able to speak. "Gregory, I thought you were dead! And Roxy—you knew?"

Roxy stops laughing. "Gregory said you liked to be scared. So, I helped him scare you."

You ball your hands into fists, wanting to yell at Gregory, to chew him out for his mean prank.

Instead, you say nothing more and run away.

➤ **TURN TO PAGE 168.**

That's it, you've had enough of the Pizzaplex! You keep running toward the stairs, barreling down them. Behind you, the sound of Freddy snarling is growing louder. Poor Gregory, you can't believe Freddy would . . .

You can't think about it. Nearly tumbling all the way down, you make it to the bottom of the stairs, where Roxy stops suddenly.

"Wait, Cassie." She grabs your arm. "Maybe I can reason with Freddy, and find out why he's acting so wild."

She sounds confident, as if she might be able to calm down Freddy. But after what *you* saw, you aren't willing to risk it. You pull away from Roxy, continuing toward the doors.

"Cassie, come back!" Roxy cries.

But you don't listen. The doors are close by now, and as soon as you reach them, you are out of here!

You're only a few steps from the door when the Reagent suddenly appears. You'd forgotten all about it! The bot gets between you and the doors, wasting no time in releasing its chemicals. You try to retreat, but the noxious cloud envelops you, burning its way down your throat.

Roxy. You try to call her name, but all you can do is cough. Stumbling, you fall to the floor, rolling on your back as the Reagent slowly makes its way over to where you lie.

Then, everything goes dark.

GAME OVER

➤ TO START FROM THE BEGINNING, TURN TO PAGE 3.
➤ TO TRY THIS NIGHT AGAIN, TURN TO PAGE 118.

You decide you might as well take the most direct way out of the Pizzaplex. This means heading for the front entrance in the lobby.

"Let's go," you say to Roxy. "But be ready to run if the Reagent shows up."

Roxy nods. "I'm with you, Cassie. Let's get you out of here!"

You smile, grateful to have Roxy with you. With her, you feel much safer than when you were alone. Still, having her doesn't mean the danger from the Reagent is gone. You'll still have to be vigilant to avoid it.

Moving quickly but quietly, you make your way down the hall and back into the main part of the Pizzaplex. In the low neon light, it feels even emptier than usual. And more dangerous. This is definitely not your usual playground with Gregory. Where is he? You hope he has avoided the Reagent, or that he and Freddy are still working on a way to stop it.

Surprisingly, your path is clear, and you're feeling hopeful about making it to the front entrance unseen.

Until you reach the top of the stairs. A flash of movement catches your eye below; quickly, you crouch behind a planter. It's the bot! Moving slowly, it's sweeping the Pizzaplex as it hunts for organic material. And right now, it's blocking your way out.

Luckily, it doesn't seem to be looking your way. You could stay the course, wait for it to move on, then keep going to the front doors. Or you could try circumventing it, remaining on the upper level of the Pizzaplex. You look up at Roxy and press a finger to your lips, indicating for her to remain quiet while you figure out what to do.

- **IF YOU WANT TO WAIT FOR THE REAGENT TO MOVE ON, TURN TO PAGE 154.**
- **IF YOU WANT TO TRY CIRCUMVENTING THE REAGENT, TURN TO PAGE 156.**

You don't want to risk running into the Reagent as you go through the lobby to the main entrance, so you decide on the Loading Dock instead, where there are doors, plenty of them, that go outside. It's probably the least likely place for the Reagent to be. You head in that direction, Roxy staying close behind, and you make sure to go slow and check around every corner for the Reagent. You see a few security bots making their rounds, and some cleaning bots, too, but otherwise the Pizzaplex is as empty and quiet as every other night. You wonder where Gregory is right now. Is he still around somewhere? You hope the Reagent hasn't found him, or that he and Freddy are figuring out a way to stop it.

You reach the stairs that lead down to the Loading Dock and pause at the top of them. It's dark below—*really* dark. Not the kind of dark you want to be wandering around in. You press the light control set into the wall, but nothing happens.

Roxy tries, too. "It's not working."

Apparently, you don't have a choice about the pitch-black path ahead. You chew the inside of your lip, nervous, but it's not like the dark can hurt you. And you're so close to the exit. You take a deep breath and stand a little straighter, summoning your courage. A flashlight would be helpful right now, but you'll go ahead if you have to.

- **IF YOU HAVE THE FLASHLIGHT AND WANT TO USE IT, TURN TO PAGE 146.**
- **IF YOU WANT TO PROCEED INTO THE DARK, TURN TO PAGE 147.**

You suddenly remember the flashlight you found earlier. Pulling it from your bag, you flick it on. A bright stream of light emanates, strong enough to illuminate the stairs all the way to the bottom. Slowly, you make your way down, Roxy behind you, straining your ears for any sounds coming from below. You don't hear anything, but that doesn't mean much. You already know the Reagent can be sneaky. Maybe it's lying in wait for you.

But hopefully not.

You're almost at the bottom of the stairs when you pause. You don't have a great view from here, but you have two options to proceed: left or right.

The problem is, you don't know which way will be the quickest route to an exit.

You look back at Roxy, but she shrugs. You're on your own to decide which way to go.

- **IF YOU WANT TO CHECK TO THE LEFT AT THE BOTTOM OF THE STAIRS, TURN TO PAGE 149.**
- **IF YOU WANT TO CHECK TO THE RIGHT AT THE BOTTOM OF THE STAIRS, TURN TO PAGE 151.**

You're hesitant to proceed in the dark, but with the Reagent on your tail, you're ready to do anything to get out of the Pizzaplex alive.

"Roxy, stay close," you say, heading down the steps. One by one, you descend until you reach the bottom, where the neon light from above barely reaches. Without being able to see where you are going, you'll have to proceed carefully, feeling your way through.

"I don't know about this," Roxy says, concerned.

"I know." You don't know about it, either. "But I've got to find a way out of here." You take a few cautious steps in front of you, arms held out. Your fingers brush against something that feels like boxes. You make your way around the object, getting a little farther before your hand touches what feels like a chain-link storage lockup. You follow it, inching along, ears straining for any noises. But all you can hear is Roxy, moving cautiously behind you.

You pause, spotting a red glow ahead. You wait, but it doesn't move, so you take a few more steps toward it. Hope fills you as an EXIT sign slides into view. It must be a door to the outside!

You start for it, then freeze. The lit sign flickers for a moment as a dark shadow moves across it. There's something else down here with you!

You turn back to Roxy. "Run!" You don't wait, darting past her, back in the direction of the stairs.

"Wait, Cassie!" Roxy calls. "It could be a cleaning bot, or—"

You don't wait to hear more, not willing to risk it as you reach the stairs again and fly back up them. You're almost to the top when a dark form appears, blocking your way.

The Reagent.

You freeze, ready to turn back, but the Reagent is too fast. It raises its arms and lets its chemicals loose. You try to scream for Roxy, but the thick, noxious mist chokes you instantly.

It's too late.

Your limbs go loose, and the last thing you see before the dark closes in is the bottom of the stairs, rushing up at you.

GAME OVER

➤ TO START FROM THE BEGINNING, TURN TO PAGE 3.
➤ TO TRY THIS NIGHT AGAIN, TURN TO PAGE 118.

You creep down to the bottom of the stairs. Using the flashlight, you illuminate the area to the left of them, sweeping carefully through the dark space crowded with all sorts of crates and boxes. At first, everything looks clear. Then, suddenly, you see a bit of movement in the distance. You train the flashlight on it, then immediately pull the light away.

It's the Reagent! It's sweeping the Loading Dock area.

Fortunately, it didn't see you.

"Roxy, it's down there!" you whisper, pushing past her. "We have to get out of here!"

As quickly and quietly as you can, you run back up the stairs and into the main area of the Pizzaplex. Panicking, you don't pay close attention to where you are headed. You just want to put as much distance between you and the Reagent as possible.

"Cassie," Roxy calls after you. "Slow down. Wait!"

You finally slow your steps, allowing Roxy to catch up as you two make your way to the Prize Counter. But before you or she can say anything else, you spot something else: Gregory and Freddy.

You start to cry out to Gregory, but pause. Something strange is going on. Gregory and Freddy appear to be having a heated conversation, though you can't hear what they are saying. All you know is that Freddy is looking increasingly angry.

Suddenly, Freddy raises his arms, claws out, and grabs Gregory.

"Cassie, don't look!" Roxy throws a hand over your eyes, so you don't see what happens. But you do hear the noise Gregory makes, one that twists your stomach into a knot. When you manage to pull Roxy's hand away, a terrible sight awaits you: Freddy holding a now-limp Gregory.

Your friend is dead. You manage to stop your scream from coming out full force, but a strangled squeak still escapes.

Freddy's head snaps in your direction. He spots you, baring his teeth in a snarl, and bolts straight for you.

"Run!" you yell to Roxy.

She obeys, following you, but you don't know which way to go. You could run to Roxy's greenroom and barricade the door. Or for the main entrance, which is probably the way you should have gone in the first place. You could also try to make a stand . . . if only Roxy was equipped to deal with Freddy!

- **IF YOU WANT TO RETREAT TO ROXY'S GREENROOM, TURN TO PAGE 141.**
- **IF YOU WANT TO RUN TO THE MAIN ENTRANCE, TURN TO PAGE 143.**
- **IF ROXY HAS MONTY'S CLAWS AND YOU WANT HER TO FIGHT FREDDY, TURN TO PAGE 152.**

Moving slowly and silently, you make your way to the bottom of the stairs and shine the flashlight to the right. The Loading Dock reminds you a little of a maze, though there isn't much to see, mostly a lot of tools and equipment, plus boxes and crates of all sizes. Sweeping the beam of light around, you search, eyes peeled for any hint of movement.

But you don't see any. Instead, you spot something way better: a door with an EXIT sign hanging over it!

It's not far from the stairs, though there are a lot of boxes nearby, making it hard to tell if anything is close. But nothing ventured, nothing gained. All you want to do is get out of the Pizzaplex.

"Let me go first," says Roxy. "In case anything is there."

"Good idea."

You let the animatronic get ahead of you. Roxy can move pretty quietly for being so big, and you're impressed at how easily she slips between the piles of boxes. You make your way across the Loading Dock, the exit door getting so close you swear you can smell fresh air already.

Then, there's a sound behind you, like metal against metal. You spin, raising the flashlight.

The Reagent is merely steps behind.

You start to yell, to call out for Roxy, but it raises its arms before you can, chemicals spraying directly at you. Immediately, you can't breathe, and your eyes burn like they are on fire.

You drop the flashlight, which goes out, leaving the dark to close in on you.

GAME OVER

➤ TO START FROM THE BEGINNING, TURN TO PAGE 3.
➤ TO TRY THIS NIGHT AGAIN, TURN TO PAGE 118.

You stop as you remember that Roxy is equipped with Monty's Claws. That should make her more than a match for Freddy!

"Roxy!" you cry. "Stop Freddy! Use your new claws!"

Roxy pauses when you do, looking down at her newly upgraded arms. Then, she smiles and turns back to Freddy, who is still charging at you, roaring. "I've got this!"

Freddy doesn't slow, but Roxy dodges out of the way, raking her claws across Freddy's side as he passes. Freddy lets out a cry, spinning toward Roxy as he tries to grab her. But Roxy jumps back, keeping out of his reach as he grabs again and again.

"You've got him!" you cry, swelling with admiration for your favorite member of the Glamrock group. With Monty's Claws, Roxy is unstoppable.

Growling, Freddy lunges again, but Roxy doesn't flinch. She rakes her claws across him again. They bite even deeper this time, and Freddy stumbles, falling to the ground. He twitches a little but doesn't get up. You let out a cry of triumph!

"Roxy! Why did you do that?" Suddenly, you hear a voice that you never expected to hear again.

You turn as Gregory comes running up, very much alive.

"You ruined the whole joke!" he continues.

"What?" You don't understand.

"Oh," says Roxy, chastised. "I guess I got carried away."

"I'll say," says Freddy weakly.

Your stomach drops. "This was another joke?"

"Duh!" says Gregory. "Roxy was supposed to get you to—"

"*You* were in on it?" you say to Roxy, horrified.

Roxy nods. "We were trying to scare you. Gregory said you like to be scared."

You frown, feeling sicker than ever. All this time, Roxy wasn't on your side at all. She was just following Gregory's orders.

"C'mon, Cassie." Gregory grins at you. "It was supposed to be funny!"

But you're not laughing. Tears fill your eyes. Before anyone can say anything else, you turn and run away.

➤ **TURN TO PAGE 168.**

As desperate as you are to get out of the Pizzaplex, you decide patience is the way to go. Still crouched, you and Roxy wait and watch as the Regent continues its sweep below. After what seems like forever, it finally moves on, rolling out of view. You wait a little longer, just to make sure it's really gone, then cautiously get up.

"C'mon," you say to Roxy.

"I'm right behind you, Cassie."

Silently as possible, you creep down the stairs until you reach the lobby area. There's still no sign of the Reagent, emboldening you. The front entrance is in sight, which means you are only steps from safely escaping the Pizzaplex. You start across the lobby, the large fountain of Freddy looming over you as you pass.

Suddenly, there's movement around the side of the fountain. You jump, then catch yourself. It's only a cleaning bot, not the Reagent. But the moment the cleaning bot spots you, it starts making loud noises as if it's spotted a mess it really wants to clean up.

"Roxy!" Your chest tightens at the noise. "Chase it away!"

"I'm on it!"

Roxy runs at the bot, which retreats, heading toward the other areas of the Pizzaplex with Roxy on its heels. This is your chance. You make a run for the front doors, not caring how much noise your sneakers make as they slap against the tile floor of the lobby. The doors get closer, closer . . .

A large shape cuts in front of you and you skid to a stop a few feet from it.

The Reagent! It must have been drawn back to the lobby by the cleaning bot's noises.

There's no time to think. You spin, intent on retreating, but you make it only a couple of steps before a cloud of chemicals envelops you. This close, the burning sensation is even worse than last night, choking you before you can cry out. Your sight blurs as tears fill your eyes, and within moments, your limbs go weak. You try to run, but it's no good. You fall to the floor, your vision going murky.

The last thing you see is the Reagent rolling forward, still spraying chemicals, until it is right above you.

Then, everything goes dark.

GAME OVER

> TO START FROM THE BEGINNING, TURN TO PAGE 3.

> TO TRY THIS NIGHT AGAIN, TURN TO PAGE 118.

You definitely can't go down the stairs with the Reagent in the lobby, so you decide to stay upstairs and try to go around the murderous machine. You wave a hand at Roxy, who follows quietly as you leave the stairs behind to look for another way down to the front doors. But you don't make it far before you come across another shocking sight: Gregory and Freddy!

To your surprise, they are right out in the open, in the Prize Counter, surrounded by all the Pizzaplex stuffed animals and toys. You start to cry out to Gregory, but Roxy puts a hand on your shoulder, stopping you. It doesn't take long to understand why. You can't hear what they are saying, but Gregory and Freddy appear to be arguing. Freddy is looking angrier and angrier with each passing moment. Then, suddenly, he roars and raises his arms, claws out.

"Cassie, don't look!" Roxy grabs you, pulling you close so that you don't see what follows. But even though she shields your eyes, you still hear the scream that emanates from Gregory. You struggle against Roxy, who finally lets you go. But when you turn back, a horrible sight awaits: Gregory, totally limp in Freddy's arms.

You stifle a scream, retreating a few steps. You know you should run to get away from Freddy and whatever madness has gripped him—but if you run, he might spot you. There are some planters nearby. If you move quickly, you can hide behind them. Whatever you do, you need to do it quickly!

➤ **IF YOU WANT TO HIDE BEHIND THE PLANTERS, TURN TO PAGE 157.**

➤ **IF YOU WANT TO RUN AWAY, TURN TO PAGE 158.**

There's no time to waste. Pulling Roxy over to the cluster of planters, you duck down before Freddy looks your way. Your heart feels like it's slid up into your throat as you peek through the plastic leaves, watching as Freddy stomps around the lifeless Gregory. Why did Freddy attack him like that? You glance up at Roxy, who returns your silent question with an apprehensive look, which makes you feel even worse. Now you have to evade both the Reagent *and* Freddy.

If you don't, you're going to end up like Gregory.

The planters and fake greenery provide a good hiding place, but now you are stuck—at least until Freddy moves on and the coast is clear. You hope that's soon, even if you have no idea what to do after. But one thing is clearer than ever: if you don't get out of the Pizzaplex soon, you might never leave!

"Is Freddy still there?" Roxy whispers.

Silently, you nod.

"There are too many plants. I can't see." Roxy shifts, trying to move into a better position. As she does, she accidentally snags your bag, pulling it off your shoulder. It falls to the floor and opens, spilling stuff with a clatter that makes your teeth clench. You scoop the items and the bag back up, but it's too late. When you look back through the leaves, Freddy is staring directly at you.

He's spotted you!

With only a split second to think, you have to make a decision. Run away, and hope Freddy can't catch you? Or—you glance up at Roxy—make a stand here, and try to stop Freddy for good. But is Roxy equipped for a battle like that?

➤ IF YOU WANT TO RUN, TURN TO PAGE 159.

➤ IF ROXY HAS MONTY'S CLAWS AND YOU WANT HER HELP TO DEAL WITH FREDDY, TURN TO PAGE 160.

After what Freddy did to Gregory, you need to get out of here, fast!

"Run!" you whisper to Roxy before taking off. You hear Roxy's steps behind you as you bolt away from the Prize Counter. But then, you hear something else . . .

It's Freddy, roaring monstrously. He's spotted you!

"Faster, Cassie!" Roxy cries.

You quicken your step, heart pounding as you run through the Pizzaplex. You know you can't outrun Freddy forever. Already, you can hear him getting closer, and if you are going to get away from him, you're going to have to be smart.

You and Roxy reach the top of the lobby stairs. You pause for a moment, not sure where to go next. If you keep heading toward the backstage area, maybe you can lose Freddy. Or you can run down the stairs and try to reach the main entrance; if you can get outside, Freddy can't follow. Then, you look at Roxy. She may not be acting wild like Freddy, but if she was equipped for it, maybe she could make a stand against him? Roxy waits, glancing anxiously behind you as you try to decide.

- **IF YOU WANT TO HEAD TO THE BACKSTAGE AREA, TURN TO PAGE 162.**
- **IF YOU WANT TO RUN FOR THE MAIN ENTRANCE, TURN TO PAGE 164.**
- **IF ROXY HAS MONTY'S CLAWS AND YOU WANT HER HELP TO DEAL WITH FREDDY, TURN TO PAGE 166.**

You can't stand up against Freddy, so there's only one other choice: run.

You bolt away, not waiting for Roxy as panic grips you. Whatever is wrong with Freddy, it's bad enough to have caused him to attack Gregory. You have no doubt that he will do the same thing to you if he manages to catch up!

Your heart pounds as you bolt back through the Pizzaplex, past the stairs, and into the mainstage area. You don't know where you are going, only that you need to get away from Freddy and find a place to hide. Footsteps sound behind you, but you're too afraid to look back. Maybe it's Roxy—but maybe it's Freddy. If you slow down even a little bit, it might give him the chance to grab you.

You skid across the tile floor, barely making a turn, then dart down a hallway.

Suddenly, a dark shape rolls into view, blocking your way. You stumble, nearly colliding with it.

The Reagent!

You don't even have time to turn before it raises its arm and releases its chemicals. The cloud hits you directly, burning your eyes and nose even worse than the night before. Still, you try to run.

But you don't make it far. Within a few steps, your limbs begin to seize up and you fall to the floor. Stuck on your back, you stare up at the ceiling, struggling to breathe as the Reagent slowly rolls into your view.

Then, the dark overcomes you.

GAME OVER

➤ TO START FROM THE BEGINNING, TURN TO PAGE 3.
➤ TO TRY THIS NIGHT AGAIN, TURN TO PAGE 118.

When you glance at Roxy, you remember the new arms—and their claws—that you found for her in the crate. With those, she should be able to take on Freddy!

"Roxy!" You point at her recent upgrades. "We'll never run away in time. You need to fight Freddy!"

Roxy looks down at the claws and flexes her fingers. "Oh, right! Stand back, Cassie. I've got this!"

Roxy steps out of the plants as Freddy comes roaring at you, looking wild. He grabs at Roxy, but she dodges him, digging her claws into his shoulder as she does. You hear the scream of tearing metal. But the damage doesn't seem to slow Freddy down. With another bloodcurdling roar, he spins and lunges at Roxy again. She dances out of the way easily and grabs him by the shoulders, digging her claws in deep. You hear a *crunch* as Freddy stumbles, falling to the ground. He still looks awake, and his limbs are twitching, but he doesn't get up. Relief floods you. Roxy must have damaged something that controlled his movements.

Then, you hear a voice cry: "Roxy! That wasn't part of the plan!"

You spin as Gregory comes running up—a very alive Gregory.

"What?" You don't understand. A moment ago, you were sure that he was dead. "Part of what plan?"

Roxy comes over beside you, head hanging. "Sorry, Gregory. I guess I got carried away."

On the floor, Freddy tries to get up and fails. "I agree, Roxy." He sounds normal again.

That's when you understand. "This was all another joke?"

Gregory grins and shrugs. "Can you blame me? Roxy was supposed to get you to—"

"What?" you cry, turning to Roxy. It feels like the floor is dropping out from below you. "Roxy, you were in on this?"

"Gregory said you like to be scared," Roxy explains. "Didn't you have fun?"

"No!" Tears fill your eyes. All this time, Roxy wasn't on your side at all. She was just part of another one of Gregory's pranks.

"Don't be such a spoilsport," says Gregory. "It was awesome!"

It wasn't awesome for you. You want to scream that at Gregory, and at Roxy and Freddy, but the words get stuck in your throat. Instead, you turn on your heel and run away.

➤ **TURN TO PAGE 168.**

Freddy is closing in, and you decide to keep going toward the backstage area. You start running again, searching for a good place to hide as you do. Then, you spot it: the Glamrock Beauty Salon! It's shut up at night; there's no reason for Freddy to look for you there. You run for the entrance, passing beneath the giant neon scissors. The front is filled with glass windows, but it's dark enough that Freddy shouldn't spot you if you duck behind something. Inside, you hide behind one of the swivel chairs at a hairdresser station.

"Roxy, hide over there!" you whisper, pointing at a dark corner out of view of the front windows. Roxy obeys, making herself as small as possible for a giant animatronic.

Then, you wait, keeping silent. Minutes pass with no Freddy, and you start to relax. He must have gone to another part of the Pizzaplex looking for you. Maybe if you move quickly, you can double back and go out the front door before he returns. You wave to get Roxy's attention, gesturing for her to go closer to the windows and make sure Freddy isn't in view outside. But she doesn't understand. She shrugs, her arm catching the edge of a table covered in hair products as she does. The bottles and jars clatter to the floor.

You duck back down behind the chair. Did Freddy hear that? Your heart drops as you hear a sound somewhere outside the salon. You can't help it; you peek around the chair. A dark figure fills the door, but it's not Freddy.

It's the Reagent! You were followed.

A gasp escapes you, and the bot swivels in your direction. It's spotted you! You jump up, but there's nowhere to run as the Reagent charges, spraying its chemicals directly at you.

"Roxy!" you gasp, but within moments, you can hardly breathe. The chemicals burn your eyes and throat, and though you stumble toward the exit, the Reagent keeps spraying until the air is so filled with the viscous cloud that you can hardly see. You think you hear Roxy coming for you, but everything is getting fuzzy.

Then, the floor rushes up at you, and the world goes dark.

GAME OVER

➤ TO START FROM THE BEGINNING, TURN TO PAGE 3.
➤ TO TRY THIS NIGHT AGAIN, TURN TO PAGE 118.

After watching what Freddy did to Gregory, the only thing you want right now is to get out of the Pizzaplex in one piece. So, you run down the stairs, heading for the main entrance.

Roxy follows after. "Freddy is getting closer!" she warns.

You try to pick up the pace, but your heart is already pounding and you're gasping for breath. Still, the doors are getting closer. You reach the lobby, bolting past the Freddy fountain, solely focused on your avenue of escape. Behind you, there are angry growls and snarls, unlike anything you've ever heard from Freddy before. You can't believe what happened to Gregory, and you don't understand why, but there's no way you're going to try to figure it out now.

Finally, you reach the doors, colliding with the closest one as you try to open it and escape.

But the door doesn't budge.

You try it again and again, but it refuses to open.

"It's locked!" you cry desperately at Roxy, who also tries, but it doesn't move for her any more than it does for you.

It doesn't matter. You lost your chance. Freddy barrels down on you, shoving Roxy out of the way and raising his claws.

You scream.

But instead of attacking, Freddy's chest suddenly bursts open. Inside sits Gregory—a very alive Gregory—who is laughing hysterically. Freddy straightens and joins him.

But worse than that, so does Roxy.

You get to your feet, fuming with anger and embarrassment. "This was another prank? You promised you'd stop, Gregory!"

Still laughing, he shrugs. "I couldn't resist. Especially with Roxy's help. We really got you, Cassie!"

You look at Roxy. "You were in on this the whole time?"

Roxy grins. "Gregory said you like to be scared. Did you have fun, Cassie?"

"No!" you cry, unable to contain your rage any longer. "I thought

Gregory was dead and Freddy was gonna kill me next. That wasn't fun at all!"

Roxy looks a little chastised, but Gregory and Freddy are still laughing. You can't deal with it anymore. Without another word, you run off, leaving all of them behind.

➤ **TURN TO PAGE 168.**

Looking at Roxy, you spot her claws: the new claws you found and equipped in Monty's greenroom. Those should make her a match for Freddy.

"Roxy!" You point at the claws. "We can't run forever!"

Roxy glances down at the claws and grins. "Stand back, Cassie. I've got this!"

And not a moment too soon. Freddy comes barreling at you, growling and snarling like a wild animal. Roxy gets between you and him, dodging as he attacks her. She claws him once on the arm, then again down the back, dancing out of the way as he tries to grab her. Growing increasingly frustrated, Freddy doesn't pay attention to where he is, getting dangerously close to the top of the stairs. He lunges at Roxy again, but she moves out of the way, her new claws biting deep into his chest.

Freddy stumbles back and you see your chance.

You run forward, shoving Freddy. Already unbalanced, he steps backward, not realizing that there's no more floor, only stairs. He flails backward and then falls, tumbling down the stairs until he reaches the bottom. There, he doesn't move.

"We did it!" Roxy cries.

But you're not sure. Not yet. Cautiously, you make your way down the stairs, Roxy at your side. Freddy remains still the whole time.

You let out a sigh of relief.

Then, suddenly, Freddy's chest pops open.

"Ow . . ." Gregory climbs out, very much alive. "That hurt . . ."

You don't understand. "I saw Freddy kill you!"

"No," says Gregory. "You only thought you did." Then, to your surprise, he turns to Roxy. "Why did you do that? You were supposed to—"

"What?" you interrupt, finally understanding. This was yet another one of Gregory's elaborate pranks. "Roxy, you were in on this?"

She nods. "Gregory said it would be fun. That you like being scared. Did you have fun, Cassie?"

You can't believe it. Roxy was working with Gregory this whole time. "No!" you cry, unable to contain your frustration any longer. "That wasn't fun at all."

"Sure it was!" Gregory chuckles. "Until the end, that is."

He doesn't get it. He *never* does. You want to yell some more, let the anger out, but instead you just blink at them for a moment, tears filling your eyes.

Then, you turn away and run.

➤ **TURN TO PAGE 168.**

NIGHT 5

It's almost nighttime again. You only know that because of the tiny window in the supply closet where you've been hiding all day. You found this spot last night and watched as the window went from dark to light, the shadows moving across the floor as the sun crossed the sky and then began to set, casting the room in warm orange tones. Now, those vibrant hues are almost gone, leaving you in the dark again. Soon, the Pizzaplex will be closed and here you still are, crying and feeling bad for yourself after what happened last night.

Gregory's behavior, you understand. His sense of humor has always been dark, even dangerous, and even though you're still furious with him over playing so many mean pranks on you, that's how he is. It's Roxy's betrayal that really stings. After she saved your birthday party, you really thought she was nice. And kind. And that she'd never play such a mean prank on you.

But she did. And it hurts.

You shift in place, your arms and legs stiff from being hidden away all day. You thought about leaving, but the last thing you wanted was to run into Gregory or Freddy—or worse, Roxy—while you did. So instead, you spent the whole day locked away in here, alone and letting your tears flow. You wipe your eyes for the hundredth time, hoping that wherever Gregory is, he feels guilty. At least a little.

But you doubt it.

Tap tap.

You turn your head toward the sound, which seems to be coming from the door to the storage closet.

Tap tap tap. This time, you know you heard it.

"Cassie?" You're surprised to hear Roxy's voice. "Are you in there?"

You frown. "Go away. I don't want to play any more games."

"I'm not playing any games," Roxy says. "I promise. Please open the door, it's important."

You want to ignore her, but the pleading sound in her voice gives you an achy feeling in your chest, so you give in, going over and letting her in. The animatronic nearly fills the small closest, but Roxy has a look on her face that makes her seem smaller than usual, somehow.

"I'm sorry," Roxy says quickly. "About last night."

You look away, unable to believe her. "Did Gregory tell you to say that? Pretend to be regretful so you can lure me out for another game?"

Roxy shakes her head. "No, Cassie, I . . . I should have known what happened wouldn't be fun for you, but I didn't." She pauses. "And I'm not sure why."

That gets your interest. You look back at Roxy. "What do you mean?"

Roxy shifts from one foot to another. "I'm not sure. Only that I don't think I am acting normal. Something is . . . off."

Some of your sadness recedes, replaced by intrigue. "Roxy, have you scanned your programming lately?"

Roxy shakes her head. "No, I haven't. But that is a good idea. Please wait." A moment later, Roxy's face goes blank as the animatronic begins an internal scan. You wait patiently for a few minutes until her features brighten again.

Immediately, she frowns. "Oh no. Cassie, you were right. My programming *has* been tampered with."

"By Gregory?"

She nods. "Yes. He altered it so that I would assist him in his prank last night. But I've found something else, too." She pauses. "Something much, much worse."

Knowing how dark Gregory's humor has gotten, you aren't sure you want to hear what's coming. But you have to know. "What did Gregory do to you, Roxy?"

"He's altering my programming so that I will turn on you, Cassie. And attack you."

A shiver runs over your skin. "When?"

Roxy hesitates for a moment. "Soon."

Anger and fear flash, chasing away the last of your sadness. But it's followed by sudden resolve. You're tired of Gregory's cruel games. But he's not the only one who knows how to reprogram the animatronics. "I'm not going to let that happen!" You stand again, pushing past Roxy and heading to the door. "C'mon, if we can get to a main computer terminal, I can get into your code and fix what Gregory changed."

Roxy doesn't move. "But Cassie, I'm not sure where the Reagent is. It might still be active in the Pizzaplex!"

Whatever Gregory has done to Roxy, there's no time to waste in undoing it. But Roxy has a point; if the Reagent is still around, you need to be careful. Part of you wants to make a run for the main computer as fast as possible, but the cautious part of you says you should move slower, taking the time to make sure the Reagent isn't around. You look up at Roxy, who waits patiently for you to decide what to do.

- **IF YOU WANT TO BE CAUTIOUS AND SEARCH THE HALLWAY CAREFULLY, TURN TO PAGE 171.**
- **IF YOU WANT TO MAKE A RUN FOR THE MAIN COMPUTER ROOM, TURN TO PAGE 172.**

With the Reagent still possibly active out there, you don't want to risk barreling through the Pizzaplex and running into it. So, with Roxy close behind, you carefully open the door to the storage room. You search both ways, but don't see anything concerning. Keeping quiet, you move out into the hallway, making your way toward the main computer room. The Pizzaplex seems quieter than usual. And darker, you realize, especially when you reach the lobby area. Most of the neon lights have gone out, leaving only a handful to illuminate your way. You look questioningly to Roxy, but she only shrugs. Is this Gregory's work? Or something to do with the Reagent's mission?

You don't have time to ponder this; suddenly, there's a bit of quick movement in the distance.

You freeze. "What was that?"

"I don't know," whispers Roxy.

You see it again, barely visible in the low light. A dark shape, like a moving shadow. Maybe it's only a cleaning or security bot, but you're too afraid to get closer, in case it spots you. Or it's something more dangerous.

"Maybe we should wait until it's gone," Roxy suggests.

However, the longer you wait, the less time you'll have to undo Roxy's programming before she turns on you. If only the lights were working normally. Or, if you had a flashlight, you could see what it is from here.

➤ IF YOU WANT TO WAIT UNTIL THE UNIDENTIFIED SHAPE MOVES ON, TURN TO PAGE 173.

➤ IF YOU HAVE THE FLASHLIGHT AND WANT TO SEE WHAT IT IS, TURN TO PAGE 174.

You decide there's no time to waste.

"We need to get to the main computer terminal," you tell Roxy, "as soon as possible!"

"Okay." She nods. "Let's go!"

You leave the storage closet behind and plunge into the hall, moving quickly. There's no time to waste. Even through you're worried about encountering the Reagent again, you don't know what Gregory did to Roxy, and you're willing to bet that it won't take long to kick in. If you don't get to the computer terminal quickly, there's no telling what will happen.

The hall seems darker than usual, a suspicion that's confirmed as you get out into public areas of the Pizzaplex. Half of the neon signs have gone dark, though you don't know why. Something to do with the Reagent? Or something Gregory did? Whatever it is, it makes your rush to get to the computer room less safe than you like. The best you can do is scan the darkness as you continue on, hoping you'll spot anything that moves before it spots you.

At the bottom of the main lobby stairs up to the mainstage, you pause for a breath. Also, the darkness above you isn't very inviting.

Roxy seems to sense your hesitance. "I think I might know another way, Cassie," she says. "There's an elevator that will take us near the main computer terminal room."

"An elevator?" That doesn't sound much better, but if it's in a less exposed part of the Pizzaplex, maybe it's not a bad idea. You glance up the stairs one more time. Then again, you're more familiar with the mainstage area, so you'll know the best way to retreat if you do run into any unexpected dangers.

➤ **IF YOU WANT TO CONTINUE UP THE STAIRS, TURN TO PAGE 189.**

➤ **IF YOU WANT TO TAKE THE ELEVATOR, TURN TO PAGE 190.**

Quietly, you watch the shadowy shape as it moves around. It makes its way through the Pizzaplex at a frustratingly slow pace, one that makes you itchy with impatience. If only you could see what it is—but the only thing you can make out is an indistinct, mysterious form. Finally, it moves off out of view, into another part of the Pizzaplex. When you're sure it's gone, you jump up, waving Roxy forward. You've wasted enough time as it is, and there's no telling how long you have before whatever Gregory did to Roxy's programming kicks in.

You're not only looking, you're listening as well, ears straining to pick up even the slightest sounds. But the Pizzaplex is almost deadly silent. You hear only yours and Roxy's faint footsteps as you make your way to the stairs.

There, Roxy pauses suddenly.

"C'mon, Roxy," you urge. "If we go this way, we'll be at the main computer terminal in no time."

Roxy seems to think for a moment. "Yes, but we don't know what's at the top of the stairs. I know an elevator. Maybe we should take that instead."

Roxy makes a good point. In the dark, you can't tell what might be waiting for you above. Taking an elevator might be risky, too, but what if it gets you closer to the main computer without having to pass through the areas of the Pizzaplex with the least amount of cover?

➤ **IF YOU WANT TO CONTINUE UP THE STAIRS, TURN TO PAGE 181.**

➤ **IF YOU WANT TO FOLLOW ROXY TO THE ELEVATOR, TURN TO PAGE 182.**

You pull out the flashlight from your bag and flick it on, shining the beam in the direction of the shape. To your relief, it's only a cleaning bot, which ignores you and continues along on its mission. You turn off the flashlight and gesture to Roxy to keep moving, making your way into the lobby and to the bottom of the stairs. You pause there, unsure of whether to proceed. The dark seems even heavier here somehow, even with a handful of the neon signs still lit, and you can't see what's above. If you make your way up the stairs and something is at the top, it might spot you before you have a chance to spot it.

You consider the flashlight again, afraid that if you use it too much, something will see the beam and come investigate. But at the same time, if it will help you see the Reagent and give you a chance to retreat, maybe you *should* utilize it.

You take a deep breath, having trouble deciding. Beside you, Roxy seems to be growing impatient. Is that because she doesn't know what to do, either? Or is she anxious about the ticking clock of Gregory's rogue programming? The only thing you're sure of is that the longer you take to decide, the more likely it is that she'll turn on you.

- **IF YOU WANT TO USE THE FLASHLIGHT AGAIN BEFORE YOU PROCEED UP THE STAIRS, TURN TO PAGE 175.**
- **IF YOU WANT TO PROCEED UP THE STAIRS IN THE DARK, TURN TO PAGE 176.**

Using the flashlight again is risky, but so is trying to traverse the stairs in the dark. You flick the light on, sweeping the beam across the steps as you carefully make your way up. You don't only trust your eyes; you also keep your ears open, listening for any sounds of movement that don't belong to you or Roxy. Behind you, Roxy sticks close, only moving when you do.

You make it to the top of the stairs and shine the light around again. But the mainstage area appears to be deserted; you don't see so much as a cleaning bot at work. Relieved, you let out the breath you'd been holding. Maybe after two nights of seeking and destroying organic material, the Reagent has finally finished its assignment and gone back into storage. You cross your fingers, hoping that's the case, and start toward the main computer room again. But you only get a few steps before you realize that Roxy isn't keeping up. She's still behind you, but moving slower than usual, her head hanging low.

"Roxy?" you ask, worried. "Is something wrong?"

Slowly, Roxy raises her head. "I . . . I think so. Cassie, I don't feel so good."

"Oh no, is it Gregory's programming?"

She nods. "I don't think you have much time left."

You tense. If time is running out, you should make a run for the computer room and try to deprogram Roxy before whatever Gregory did fully kicks in. But you don't know for sure that the Reagent is gone; if you aren't careful, you could run into it around any corner.

Roxy lets out a little groan and you know you need to make a decision—and fast!

- **IF YOU WANT TO MAKE A RUN FOR THE MAIN COMPUTER ROOM, TURN TO PAGE 177.**
- **IF YOU WANT TO CONTINUE BEING CAUTIOUS SO AS NOT TO ATTRACT THE REAGENT, TURN TO PAGE 179.**

You don't want to risk using the flashlight again, so you go up the stairs in the dark. You take the steps slowly, pausing repeatedly to see if you can hear anything moving above. But it remains silent as you ascend, finally reaching the top. You look around, trying to spot any movement, but the mainstage area is totally deserted, and you don't see so much as a cleaning bot making its way around. *Thank goodness*, you think. Maybe the Reagent finally completed its task and has gone back into storage. After all, it's had a couple of nights to clear all the organic material out of the Pizzaplex.

But you should still be cautious. You start toward the main computer room, only to realize after a couple of steps that Roxy isn't behind you.

"Roxy?" you whisper, going back to the stairs. When you look down them, it's like looking into a deep, dark pool. All you can see at the bottom is a vague outline of the animatronic, standing perfectly still. "Roxy?"

"I'm sorry, Cassie."

Roxy speaks so quietly, you can barely hear her.

You tremble. "Why?"

Suddenly, a pair of eyes lights up below. They're Roxy's eyes . . . but they look different than before. She snarls, then suddenly surges forward, bolting up the stairs, directly at you.

You have just enough time to scream before Roxy reaches you.

GAME OVER

➤ TO START FROM THE BEGINNING, TURN TO PAGE 3.

➤ TO TRY THIS NIGHT AGAIN, TURN TO PAGE 168.

There's no time to waste. Whatever Gregory did is clearly beginning to affect Roxy, which means you need to get her to a main computer terminal as quickly as possible!

"C'mon, Roxy!" you say. "We need to move fast!"

You take off in a run, turning off the flashlight. You may not have time to be cautious, but that doesn't mean you should be foolish and let yourself be spotted by any bot that might be roaming around. You run though the Pizzaplex, determined not to let Gregory get the best of you this time. And not to let his programming take Roxy away from you. Now that you know she's on your side, and only participated in Gregory's pranks because he made her, you can't let that stand!

You push yourself a little harder, but the moment you do, your foot comes down on something.

"Ah!" You feel a *crunch*, followed by a stab of pain. You flail and fall, landing hard on the Pizzaplex floor.

"Cassie, are you okay?!" Roxy rushes to your side, but it's too late. You are definitely *not* okay. There's just enough light for you to see an empty, crushed can of Sodaroni lying nearby. But it's your ankle that's concerning you right now. It hurts a lot, and when you try to get up, you stumble.

You frown. "I think I sprained it!"

"Oh no!" Roxy helps lift you. "Can you keep going? Lean against me, I'll help you."

There's urgency in her voice, which gives you the motivation to get up again, using Roxy to steady yourself. You hobble along like that, praying that the Reagent doesn't come rolling along. You'll never outrun it now!

Luckily, you don't encounter anything or anyone, and after a few minutes you're nearly at the main computer room.

Roxy stops.

"C'mon," you urge. "It's only a little farther. I can make it!"

But Roxy doesn't move. Slowly, her head turns your way, her eyes meeting yours. They aren't the kind eyes that looked at you a few minutes ago. These eyes you don't recognize at all. It's Gregory's programming, you realize, a cold feeling slithering into your stomach. It's kicked in fully.

Roxy bares her teeth.

Then, she attacks.

GAME OVER

> TO START FROM THE BEGINNING, TURN TO PAGE 3.
> TO TRY THIS NIGHT AGAIN, TURN TO PAGE 168.

Even with Roxy beginning to feel weird, you can't risk attracting the attention of the Reagent if it's still around. You keep moving, Roxy staying close behind you as you creep through the Pizzaplex, keeping your eyes peeled for any hint of movement. Fortunately, the whole place seems even more deserted than usual. You can't hear anything, either, only the faint tread of your steps as you make your way to the main computer room.

Finally, you reach it, pushing open the door and closing it behind you.

You let out a breath, relieved.

"Cassie," Roxy says suddenly, "look!"

You follow where she's pointing to one of the monitors mounted on the wall, which shows the Reagent. But it's not moving and seems to be back in a storage area. Another wave of relief flows over you—the Reagent has been deactivated!

"Excellent," you crow, then head for a computer terminal. "All we need to do now is undo Gregory's programming and everything will be back to normal!"

Roxy gets a queasy look on her face. "I think you should hurry with that. I'm not sure how much longer I have."

You indicate one of the control panels. "Interface there. And don't worry, I've got this."

Roxy does as she's instructed, and you begin rifling through her protocols, looking for the one that Gregory messed with. Gregory is smart, but so are you, and you find it quickly. You bring the code up on the screen, ready to fix it, but the moment you do, the screen suddenly shifts, and a question appears:

ROCK, PAPER, OR SCISSORS?

"What?" You frown. Leave it to Gregory to turn even *this* into a game. "Which one should I pick?"

Roxy shakes her head. "I don't know." Her features are twitching in a way that's disconcerting. "But I think you need to choose quickly."

➤ **IF YOU WANT TO PICK ROCK, TURN TO PAGE 184.**
➤ **IF YOU WANT TO PICK PAPER, TURN TO PAGE 186.**
➤ **IF YOU WANT TO PICK SCISSORS, TURN TO PAGE 187.**

You don't trust taking an elevator you don't know, so you continue up the stairs instead, moving quietly so as not to alert anything that might be waiting at the top of them. Roxy stays close behind you, but when you reach the floor above, you see nothing. The Pizzaplex seems even more deserted than normal. That works for you, though, as you continue through the mainstage room, heading to the room in the backstage office area where you know there's a main computer terminal. Despite the fear of running into the Reagent again, you and Roxy make it to the computer room with no issues.

Inside, there's the computer you were looking for, along with some monitors showing various areas of the Pizzaplex. To your surprise, you spot the Reagent. But it's not moving and seems to be parked in a storage area. That must mean it finished its sweep of the Pizzaplex, which is a relief. The last thing you need right now is to be dealing with that threat, too.

Roxy makes a sick, groaning noise. "I think you'd better hurry, Cassie. I'm not feeling so well."

You don't waste any more time. "You can interface there," you instruct Roxy, pointing at a port on a control panel. Roxy obeys, and with a few keystrokes, you have her protocols pulled up. Gregory is smart, but so are you; within a few minutes you find a suspect bit of programming. But as you try to go deeper into the code, the monitor suddenly flickers. A question pops up:

ROCK, PAPER, OR SCISSORS?

"Ugh," you say. "Is this another one of Gregory's games?"

"I don't know," says Roxy. She doesn't sound well at all. "Which one is the right answer?"

"I'm not sure," you respond, "but there's one way to find out!"

➤ IF YOU WANT TO PICK ROCK, TURN TO PAGE 184.

➤ IF YOU WANT TO PICK PAPER, TURN TO PAGE 186.

➤ IF YOU WANT TO PICK SCISSORS, TURN TO PAGE 187.

"Okay," you agree after considering for a moment. "If you think the elevator will get us to the main computer faster, let's go that way!"

Roxy nods. "Sounds good."

She guides you away from the stairs, toward a corridor in a far corner of the Pizzaplex lobby, where only employees go. The hall is completely dark, and you can't see if there's anything in it, but Roxy leads the way, moving carefully. In the dark, you strain your ears to hear if anyone—or anything—is in the space with you, but you hear nothing. Finally, Roxy stops at the very end of the passage; you can just barely make out a pair of wide silver doors. This must be a freight elevator, for moving large loads up and down the floors of the Pizzaplex. But based on where it is, you think Roxy is right. This should let you out right near the room with the main computer terminal!

You locate the elevator button and press it. A few moments later, the door slides open. It's dark in the elevator, with only the lights of the button panel on the inside to illuminate the space. But you don't hesitate. Having Roxy by your side makes you more confident, and it's not like you have to ride the elevator for long. You press the button for the floor you want and the elevator begins to move, ascending smoothly.

Then, suddenly, it rattles and screeches to a stop.

"What's going on?" you say.

"I'm not sure," says Roxy. "Maybe try another floor?"

You try pressing another button, but nothing happens. Confused, you press all the buttons, hoping to get the elevator moving again. Instead, the panel suddenly flashes and goes out, plunging the whole compartment into an impenetrable darkness.

"We're trapped!" you cry, your fears rising again. But you can't let them control you. You feel around for the panel. Maybe if you work on it some more . . .

"Cassie?" Roxy asks, her voice sounding gruffer than usual.

A shiver runs down your spine. "What's wrong?"

"I'm sorry . . ." Roxy's voice sounds strange. Suddenly, her eyes light up, a red glow that makes the elevator look like it's doused in blood. "But I think you're out of time . . ."

You take a step back, but you come up against the wall of the elevator.

There's nowhere to go.

The last things you see as Roxy comes toward you are those crimson eyes, burning in the darkness.

GAME OVER

➤ TO START FROM THE BEGINNING, TURN TO PAGE 3.

➤ TO TRY THIS NIGHT AGAIN, TURN TO PAGE 168.

You hate that Gregory has turned this into a game, too, but you don't have time to figure out a way around it. Paper . . . scissors . . . you consider all the options.

But Roxanne Wolf doesn't play with paper or scissors.

Roxanne Wolf likes to *rock*.

You type the answer into the computer terminal and press the key to submit it. The screen flickers for a moment, then goes dark.

"Did it work?" you wonder aloud. Then, a spray of colors appears on the monitor—fireworks, exploding in a variety of vibrant hues. A pair of words appear in their midst: *GOOD CHOICE*.

"You did it!" cries Roxy. "Something has shifted in my programming. Whatever Gregory did, it's undone. I'm not going to turn on you anymore."

You lean back in the chair. "Thank goodness!"

But your celebration is short-lived. Suddenly, an alert pops up on the computer screen, a warning that flashes red.

"What the heck?!" You lean close again as a camera view appears on the computer. You recognize it in a heartbeat: It's the Reagent in its storage area. But as you watch, it comes back to life, arms flailing briefly before it starts rolling again, quickly and with purpose. It disappears from the camera view.

NEW MISSION. The words pop up on the screen, as red as blood. *SOLE TARGET*.

And then: *CASSIE*.

Your picture appears on the monitor, a red *X* plastered across it.

"Oh no!" you cry.

"That's not good," says Roxy. "It's not going to stop until it finds you, Cassie."

You're not going to let it get you easily. "Roxy, can you help me now? If we can find a way to stop the Reagent, or destroy it, I can escape!"

Roxy puts an arm on your shoulder. "Anything you need, Cassie. I've got your back."

You swell with hope and pride as you consider how to stop the Reagent and foil its newly assigned mission. Roxy might be able to stand up to the bot if she was equipped properly. But you can also try luring the Reagent somewhere that gives you a chance to deal with it. The main lobby? The kitchen? Roxy Raceway? A number of options occur to you, but one thing is clear: you need to confront the Reagent and destroy it, before it can destroy you!

- **IF YOU WANT TO LURE THE REAGENT TO THE MAIN LOBBY, TURN TO PAGE 199.**
- **IF YOU WANT TO LURE THE REAGENT TO THE KITCHEN, TURN TO PAGE 201.**
- **IF YOU WANT TO LURE THE REAGENT TO ROXY RACEWAY, TURN TO PAGE 203.**
- **IF ROXY IS EQUIPPED WITH MONTY'S CLAWS AND YOU WANT TO DIRECTLY CONFRONT THE REAGENT, TURN TO PAGE 213.**

You remember playing Rock, Paper, Scissors with other kids in the past. But unlike those games, there's no one else with you here, hand out, ready to throw their choice. Unless you count the absent Gregory. Leave it to him to turn this into a game as well.

Thinking carefully, you finally decide.

> PAPER, you respond, and hit the SUBMIT key.

A moment later, the computer screen goes dark. The computer is still on, but there's nothing to see, and tapping the keys on the keyboard doesn't do anything. You let out a noise of frustration. When you find Gregory, you are going to give him a big piece of your mind. He might think this is funny, but he's the only one laughing.

"I can't tell if it worked," you say. But Roxy doesn't respond. "Roxy." You turn. "Do you feel any—"

Behind you, the Roxy you knew is gone. A wild-eyed, snarling animatronic wolf is standing in her place, staring at you like you're a piece of fresh meat.

"R-R-Roxy?" you stutter, a cold bead of sweat running down your back. "Roxy, can you hear me?"

Still, she says nothing, only glares at you with blood-red eyes.

Those eyes are the last thing you see before she lunges for you.

GAME OVER

> TO START FROM THE BEGINNING, TURN TO PAGE 3.

> TO TRY THIS NIGHT AGAIN, TURN TO PAGE 168.

There's no telling which answer is the right one, and annoyance floods through you as you consider the choices at hand. This is just like Gregory, turning something serious—and dangerous—into a game. If you find him again, you're going to give him a piece of your mind, especially about messing around with Roxy's programming.

But you have to deal with this first.

›SCISSORS, you respond, and hit the SUBMIT key.

A moment later, the screen begins to flicker.

"What?" You have no idea what's going on. "Did it work? Roxy, do you feel any different?"

"I . . . I'm not sure," she replies.

Suddenly, a camera view pops up on the screen. It's the same one that shows the Reagent, back in storage. But as you watch, it comes to life again, arms flailing briefly before it rolls out of view of the camera. The screen flickers again, showing another camera's perspective—a hallway outside the storage area. The Reagent rolls down it, moving quickly, and seemingly with purpose. The screen changes a few more times and eventually you realize where the bot is headed: directly toward you!

You jump up. "We have to get out of here!"

You run for the door, but only make it a couple steps before Roxy suddenly grabs you, lifting you off the floor.

"Roxy, what are you doing?"

"I'm sorry, Cassie." She sounds genuinely concerned, though her grip tightens. "I'm trying to fight my programming, but I'm afraid I'm not having any luck."

You struggle, fear growing with every second. Not only has Roxy turned on you, the Reagent is getting closer with every second. "Please, Roxy! Let me down! I have to get out of here right now!"

But Roxy doesn't budge. "I'm sorry," she says again. "I'm really, really sorry."

The door to the computer room opens. You go limp as the Reagent rolls in, arms raised.

"Roxy . . . please," you plead, already knowing that it's hopeless.

"I'm sorry . . ." you hear one last time as the Reagent raises its arms and begins spraying you with chemicals.

GAME OVER

➤ TO START FROM THE BEGINNING, TURN TO PAGE 3.

➤ TO TRY THIS NIGHT AGAIN, TURN TO PAGE 168.

"I think we should keep going here," you say to Roxy, pointing up the stairs. You don't trust an unfamiliar elevator, and getting caught in such a small space is the last thing you want to do right now. "But let's be careful."

Slowly, you creep up the stairs, undaunted by the dark. You listen closely, hoping to catch the sound of anything above you, but the Pizzaplex seems even quieter than usual. Between the darkness and the silence, it's a lot less fun than you remember.

You reach the top of the stairs and freeze immediately, spotting movement in the distance.

"Get down!" You and Roxy crouch, waiting and watching.

At first, all you can see is a shadowy form, but then it moves closer. You let out a relieved breath. It's only a cleaning bot. After another minute, it moves on, disappearing toward another part of the Pizzaplex. You continue, Roxy staying close as you traverse the mainstage, into the backstage area. Finally, you reach the hallway with the computer room.

Roxy slows, stumbling a little.

"What's the matter?" you ask.

"I'm not sure," says Roxy. "I'm not feeling so well. I think we need to hurry, Cassie."

It must be Gregory's programming. It could fully kick in at any moment. You glance back down the hall. It's really dark, and you're nervous about heading down it without knowing what's there. If you had a flashlight, you could risk checking it out. But you're not sure you can wait, not with whatever is happening to Roxy.

➤ IF YOU HAVE THE FLASHLIGHT AND WANT TO CHECK THE HALL, TURN TO PAGE 192.

➤ IF YOU WANT TO GO IMMEDIATELY TO THE MAIN COMPUTER ROOM DESPITE THE DARK, TURN TO PAGE 193.

"Okay," you say to Roxy. "Let's take the elevator."

Roxy grins. "Follow me!"

She leads you to a far corner of the Pizzaplex, to a remote hallway that's only for bots and employees. It's pitch-black, though, and you hesitate to enter. There's no telling what might be down there, and just because you haven't seen any evidence of the Reagent, doesn't mean it's not still out there somewhere.

"I'm not sure about this," you say.

Roxy puts a supportive hand on your shoulder. "I know, but I'll be with you." She pauses. "And I don't think we should waste any time."

"Why?"

Roxy frowns. "I'm . . . I'm starting to feel funny, Cassie."

That can't be good. "Okay, let's go."

With Roxy at your side, you head down the hallway, letting the darkness swallow you. It's so dark you can barely see the animatronic's large form beside you, and you run a hand along one wall to help you keep your bearings. Finally, you reach the end of the hall, where you feel around until you locate the elevator button. There's a *ding* as the door opens, and suddenly you can see. Not well, though; the elevator is only lit by the control panel. Still, it's better than nothing. You and Roxy go inside and you press the button for the floor with the computer room. The elevator begins to ascend. You breathe a sigh of relief. One step closer to fixing Roxy.

As you approach your floor, you begin to hear strange noises.

"What's that?"

"I don't know," says Roxy.

They're getting louder. And closer. A moment before the elevator doors open again, you lunge for the HOLD button, so the door remains closed.

"Is it the Reagent?" As you listen, the noises dwindle.

Then a scratching sound begins. Right outside the elevator door. It's slow, deliberate. Whatever it is, you're pretty sure you don't want to come face-to-face with it. But the elevator door will only stay closed as long as you keep pressing the button.

You're trapped.

"Roxy, what do we do?" you say as the scratching continues. She doesn't respond. "Roxy?"

When you turn, Roxy is staring at you. But she doesn't look like the Roxy you know. Her eyes glow red, and her teeth are bared.

"C-C-Cassie . . ." She seems to have trouble speaking. "It's . . . t-t-too l-l-late." A growl escapes her. "I'm s-sorry, Cassie."

Your finger drops from the button a moment before Roxy attacks.

GAME OVER

➤ TO START FROM THE BEGINNING, TURN TO PAGE 3.
➤ TO TRY THIS NIGHT AGAIN, TURN TO PAGE 168.

Leaning carefully around the corner, you flick the flashlight on and shine it down the hallway. There's a flurry of movement. Your heart jumps into your throat, but only for a moment. It's just a cleaning bot. Spooked by your light, it goes rolling off, opting to pick another part of the Pizzaplex to clean up.

Thank goodness!

You wave Roxy forward and head down the hall, to the door leading into the main computer room. On the wall inside there are a bunch of monitors, all showing different areas of the Pizzaplex. To your surprise, you spot the Reagent on one of them. It must have completed its decontamination spree because it appears to be inactive and back in one of the storage areas. That's one problem you won't have to deal with anymore!

"Quick," you say to Roxy, "interface with the terminal there."

She obeys and you get to work, going into her programming and pulling up her protocols. Gregory is clever, but so are you, and you find his nasty work quickly. Tapping away at the keyboard, you pick apart the changes Gregory made.

"I think I've got it," you say, typing in a few last commands.

Suddenly, the screen flickers. The code disappears and a question pops up: *RED, YELLOW, OR GREEN?*

"What does that mean?" Roxy asks.

"I'm not sure." Another piece of Gregory's game, to your annoyance. But which one is the right choice? *Is* there even a right choice? You wouldn't put it beyond Gregory to ask a question with no answer.

Roxy waits patiently, trusting you to make the decision.

➤ **IF YOU WANT TO PICK RED, TURN TO PAGE 195.**

➤ **IF YOU WANT TO PICK YELLOW, TURN TO PAGE 196.**

➤ **IF YOU WANT TO PICK GREEN, TURN TO PAGE 197.**

With Roxy starting to feel strange, there's no time to be cautious.

"C'mon!" You rush down the hallway, into the dark. You can barely see, but that doesn't stop you. You know where you need to get to, and if you don't move quickly, there's no telling what will happen with Roxy. Gregory's dangerous sense of humor isn't going to mess with her, not if you can help it.

Suddenly, you collide with something big. You stumble back, startled by a menacing dark shape.

The Reagent!

You can't help it; you scream. And then you run, pushing past Roxy and back toward the mainstage area.

"Cassie!" Roxy calls after you. "Cassie, wait!"

In your panic, you barely hear her. Heart pounding and mouth dry, you run back out into the Pizzaplex, terrified as you duck behind a column to hide. You crouch down, hoping that the Reagent didn't see where you went, and that it will move on.

"Cassie?" Roxy calls out to you again, closer this time. "Cassie, where did you go? Come back out, it's safe."

Safe?

Cautiously, you move out from behind the column.

Roxy sighs, spotting you, and comes over. "You didn't need to run away. It was just a cleaning bot. It's already gone."

Relief washes over you. And then, regret. You were such a coward, running like that. "I'm sorry, Roxy. I didn't mean to run away . . . I just got scared."

"Oh, Cassie . . ."

"I won't run again. Now let's go get your programming fixed, quick!"

But Roxy doesn't move out of your way. When you look up, her eyes have turned a strange shade of red and her teeth are bared.

"S-s-sorry, Cassie," Roxy stutters, her voice half a growl. "I th-think it's t-too l-late."

You back away, but there's nowhere to go.

Roxy lets out a vicious snarl and attacks.

GAME OVER

➤ TO START FROM THE BEGINNING, TURN TO PAGE 3.
➤ TO TRY THIS NIGHT AGAIN, TURN TO PAGE 168.

You make a decision, typing in ➤RED and hitting the SUBMIT key. Code begins flashing across the screen, scrolling so quickly you don't have time to read it.

"Did it work?" asks Roxy.

"I'm not sure." The code continues to scroll as the computer makes noises, like it's doing something taxing. "Do you feel any different?"

"I will try to check my programming," Roxy says.

While she's doing that, you keep an eye on the screen, trying to catch snippets of the code to figure out what is happening. Finally, after several minutes, you attempt tapping at the keyboard again, closing out of the program, anything. But nothing seems to work. What did Gregory do? And what did you do by answering *RED* to that mysterious question?

"I don't know what's happening," you admit finally. "Roxy, have you figured anything out?"

Roxy doesn't reply. You glance up at her. She's looking straight ahead, her face devoid of emotion as she scans her programming.

"Roxy?"

She blinks—once, twice. Then, with her head moving slowly, she looks down at you.

This is not the Roxy from a few minutes ago. Her face is contorted with anger, her eyes narrowed at you, her teeth bared.

". . . Roxy?"

She snarls.

Apparently, *RED* wasn't the right answer.

A moment later, Roxy attacks.

GAME OVER

➤ **TO START FROM THE BEGINNING, TURN TO PAGE 3.**

➤ **TO TRY THIS NIGHT AGAIN, TURN TO PAGE 168.**

You have to choose one of the colors, so you type in ➤YELLOW, hitting the SUBMIT key. The screen flickers again, and a large yellow exclamation point appears, flashing, along with the words *PLEASE WAIT.*

Roxy leans over your shoulder. "Did it work?"

"I'm not sure." You obey the instruction, sitting patiently as the exclamation point continues to flash. "Do you feel like anything has changed?"

Roxy shrugs. "I will try to check my programming."

While she's doing that, you keep an eye on the screen, annoyed. This is just like Gregory, messing with you even when he's not around. You don't know what the colors mean, but you do hope that *YELLOW* is the right answer. As you watch, the exclamation point increases in speed until it's flashing so quickly that it seems to be vibrating.

Somehow, that doesn't encourage you.

"I don't know why it's doing that," you say finally. "Roxy, have you had any luck with your programming?"

"Y-yes . . ."

You glance up. Roxy's answer is the one you were hoping to hear, but the way she says it is . . . strange. "Roxy, are you okay?"

She stares straight ahead, her face devoid of any emotion. "M-my programming i-is . . . is . . ." She trails off.

"Roxy?"

Suddenly, she blinks, eyes snapping down at you. Her eyes have turned a disturbing shade of sickly yellow, and she no longer looks like the fun rock-and-roll wolf you know. She snarls, baring her teeth.

And now it's clear: *YELLOW* isn't the right answer.

A moment later, Roxy attacks.

GAME OVER

➤ TO START FROM THE BEGINNING, TURN TO PAGE 3.
➤ TO TRY THIS NIGHT AGAIN, TURN TO PAGE 168.

You look up at Roxy, and the streak of color in her hair. Might as well go with the choice Roxy likes most. You type in ➤GREEN, and hit the SUBMIT button.

Suddenly, the monitors all fill with code and begin to flash, faster and faster until they are nothing but a blur. Roxy's eyes follow the code intently, scanning it to make note of the changes being made. Then, the code disappears, leaving them all blank. A green smiley face appears on the screen in front of you.

"You did it!" Roxy exclaims. "The programming that Gregory added has been deleted."

You lean back in the chair, letting out a relieved breath. But movement catches your eye on one of the monitors. The security camera view has reappeared, showing one very particular thing: the Reagent! As you watch, it comes to life again, immediately rolling out of sight and clearly on a mission.

"Did you do that?" Roxy asks.

"I don't know!" You begin typing commands into the computer, navigating through the Pizzaplex files until you find a mention of the Reagent. What you see makes your blood turn cold. *NEW MISSION.* The words seem to fill the screen, bloody red. *SOLE TARGET.* And then: *CASSIE.*

Your picture appears on the monitor, a red *X* plastered across it.

"That's not good," says Roxy.

"No," you agree. "It definitely is not!"

"It's not going to stop until it finds you, Cassie."

"I know." But that doesn't mean you're going to let the Reagent get to you easily. "Roxy, can you help me now? If we can find a way to stop the bot or destroy it, I can escape!"

"Anything you need, Cassie." Roxy stands up straight, confidently whipping her hair back. "I've got your back. Let's turn that bot into a pile of scrap!"

You swell with hope seeing how dedicated Roxy is to helping you. But even with her at your side, it's not going to be easy. You need to come up with a plan to stop the Reagent and foil its newly assigned mission. Roxy might be able to stand up to the nasty bot if she was equipped properly. But you could also try luring the Reagent to a place where you can deal with it. The main lobby? The kitchen? The raceway? A number of options occur to you, but one thing is clear: you need to confront the Reagent and destroy it, before it can destroy you!

- **IF YOU WANT TO LURE THE REAGENT TO THE MAIN LOBBY, TURN TO PAGE 199.**
- **IF YOU WANT TO LURE THE REAGENT TO THE KITCHEN, TURN TO PAGE 201.**
- **IF YOU WANT TO LURE THE REAGENT TO ROXY RACEWAY, TURN TO PAGE 203.**
- **IF ROXY IS EQUIPPED WITH MONTY'S CLAWS AND YOU WANT TO DIRECTLY CONFRONT THE REAGENT, TURN TO PAGE 213.**

You need to deal with the Reagent once and for all. And if you're going to do that, you decide you need plenty of space to work.

Like the main lobby.

You think for a few minutes, following the Reagent's progression on the security monitors and making sure you don't lose it.

"Okay," you say to Roxy finally, "here's what we are going to do . . ."

You take a deep breath, steeling yourself. Around the corner, you can hear the Reagent rolling closer, no longer sweeping for organic material, but rather for one target and one target only: *you*. The last thing you wanted was to ever get this close to the Reagent again, but there's only one way your plan is going to work, and that's if you use yourself as bait. You only hope you're fast enough to make this work.

When you judge the Reagent is close—but not too close—you step out into the hallway.

"Hey!" You wave your arms and jump up and down. "You looking for me?"

The Reagent comes to an abrupt stop upon spotting you, then lets out a screeching noise. It raises its arms, but you start running before it has a chance to release its chemicals again. Within moments, you can hear it pursuing you. Fear pushes you to run faster, to tear through the Pizzaplex as you head to where Roxy is waiting for you: the main lobby.

Behind you, the Reagent is gaining, faster than you'd like, but a moment later you arrive at your destination. The lobby is still dark and shadowed, and you don't see Roxy, but you tell yourself that's okay. That it's part of the plan.

But you didn't count on how quickly the Reagent would gain on you. You had planned to get to the top of the stairs, but now you're not sure you have time to do so. You might need to be content with getting the Reagent to the bottom of the stairs, and trust Roxy to do the rest.

The bot is getting closer, so you need to make a decision quickly!

➤ **IF YOU WANT TO RUN TO THE TOP OF THE STAIRS, TURN TO PAGE 205.**
➤ **IF YOU WANT TO STOP AT THE BOTTOM OF THE STAIRS, TURN TO PAGE 206.**

You need to deal with the Reagent once and for all. And there's a part of you that wants payback for what it did to you in the kitchen. So that's where you decide to confront it. It will be a tight area to work, but the Reagent navigated it slower than you were able to, which makes it a good place to try to trap it.

Watching the Reagent on the monitors to make sure you know exactly where it is, you think for a few minutes. About what to do, and *how* to do it.

"Okay . . ." You get to your feet and turn to Roxy. "Here's the plan . . ."

You creep around the entrance of Chica's Mazercise, where you last saw the Reagent on the monitors. Your heart is beating hard, especially not having Roxy there with you, but you're going to have to be brave now. If you aren't, you won't stand a chance against it.

There's a sound nearby and you freeze, ready. A shadow slides into view, one you'd have to be a fool to not recognize. A moment later the Reagent appears, attached to that shadow.

It's time.

The bot is turned away from you, so you jump out from where you are lurking. "Hey! Hey, are you looking for me?"

Immediately, the Reagent spins your way, letting out a metallic screeching sound. It starts to raise its arms, but you're off and running before that happens, sneakers slapping against the Pizzaplex floor as you race across it. Behind you are the sounds of the Reagent in pursuit. And from the sound of it, it's getting closer than you'd like. You swallow hard and push yourself, moving faster as you make your way to the hall that leads to the kitchen. It's a straight shot, but by the time you reach the doors, the bot is almost upon you.

You burst through the entrance to the kitchen, hoping Roxy is ready.

Immediately, you dart to one side, running down an aisle with shelves lining the wall. As you do, you risk a glance behind. The

Reagent is so close that it can almost touch you. With one last burst of speed, you race by the shelving.

"Roxy, now!" you yell.

You hear a strained grunt as Roxy shoves one of the heavy shelves, bracing herself against the kitchen wall for leverage. You barely make it past before the whole setup comes down with a thundering crash that makes your ears ache.

The Reagent isn't so lucky. Roxy's aim is dead-on, and it lies crushed beneath the tangle of metal and cans. You wait for a moment, but it doesn't move, so you creep closer.

Suddenly, the pile shifts. You jump back. The Reagent is damaged but not destroyed. It feebly tries to raise one of its busted limbs and point a nozzle at you.

You have to do something fast. The bot's chemical tanks are exposed. Maybe if you contaminated them with something, you can make the chemicals inert. Of course, for all you know you might make them more potent. There's also something that looks like a plug; maybe you can drain the chemicals and disarm it that way?

- **IF YOU WANT TO DRAIN THE CHEMICALS FROM THE REAGENT'S TANK, TURN TO PAGE 208.**
- **IF YOU HAVE A CAN OF SODARONI AND WANT TO POUR IT INTO THE REAGENT'S TANK, TURN TO PAGE 209.**

You need to deal with the Reagent once and for all. There must be a way to defeat it before it has a chance to try to "decontaminate" you again, and you think you know the best place to try to do that: Roxy Raceway. Where better to team up with Roxy and corner the bot than on her own turf?

You watch the monitors, keeping track of the bot's movements as you ponder the best way to do what you need to do. Meanwhile, Roxy waits patiently beside you for your orders.

"Okay," you say finally. "Here's what we are going to do . . ."

"Here I am!" You stand in the mainstage area, spinning around and feeling a little silly as you yell and make a bunch of noise. "Here I am! A contaminant! Come and get me!"

You feel silly, but you're also scared. The last thing you wanted after the Reagent cornered you in the kitchen was to come face-to-face with it again. And here you are, trying to get its attention.

"Come and clean me up! I'm right here!"

Your heart jumps as you hear something, somewhere. In the low light, it's hard to see what might be approaching you. You scan the area for any hint of movement.

There! A dark form rolls into view, an outline that sends a cold shiver down your spine.

The Reagent. The moment it spots you, it freezes and lets out an angry screech. It starts to raise its nozzles, but you turn and run, not waiting around to see more. As you hoped—and feared—the Reagent immediately pursues you. Your sneakers slap against the floor of the Pizzaplex as you reach the entrance to Roxy Raceway and bolt through it. Unfortunately, the Reagent is gaining faster than you expected. It's on your heels as you reach the stairs, nearly tumbling down them as you make your way to the raceway floor.

"Roxy, get ready!" you yell.

You reach the floor and head across it to the track, climbing onto it. But you only make it a few more steps before the Reagent catches up to you. It surges past you, coming around to block your way, raising its nozzles menacingly.

A moment later, a go-kart collides with it at top speed. There's a vicious crashing sound of metal against metal and the Reagent goes flying, landing hard and skidding to a stop farther down the track.

Pulling the go-kart to one side of the track, Roxy looks back at it. "Is it dead?"

The Reagent isn't moving.

"I'm not sure," you say.

Cautiously, you approach the mangled bot that was, until a moment ago, the Reagent. It moves suddenly, causing you to jump back. The bot is damaged but unfortunately not destroyed! You can see it trying to raise its nozzle to point at you, which means you need to think fast. A panel on the Reagent's front has been smashed open, revealing its internal boards and wiring. If you had something to stab into its circuit boards, that would probably take care of it. Or maybe ripping its wires out would be good enough. Either way, you need to work fast!

- **IF YOU HAVE A SCREWDRIVER AND WANT TO STAB THE CIRCUIT BOARDS WITH IT, TURN TO PAGE 211.**
- **IF YOU TRY RIPPING OUT THE REAGENT'S WIRING, TURN TO PAGE 212.**

You can't stop now. Even with the Reagent nearly on your heels, you decide to run for the top of the stairs, where Roxy is waiting for you.

Hopefully.

You take the stairs as fast as you can, jumping them two at a time, until you are almost at the top. "Roxy! Get ready."

When you reach the last step, you stop and turn. To your horror, the Reagent is halfway up the stairs already, and closing in fast. But you ball your fists and stand your ground. The Reagent gets closer and closer, raising its limbs and aiming the nozzles toward you, until it's only a few steps away.

Suddenly, Roxy appears, a growl rumbling out of her as she throws herself at the Reagent. There's a *crunch* and the Reagent goes flying, tumbling down the steps, parts breaking and flying off it. It hits the floor of the lobby and rolls, coming to a stop against the edge of the Freddy fountain. There, it lies still.

"Is it destroyed?" says Roxy hesitantly.

"There's only one way to find out."

Hesitantly, you descend the stairs, keeping a close eye on the still form. A few weak sparks fly as you come up beside the remains, but nothing else.

"It's dead!" you cry triumphantly.

Then, the head of the Reagent—or what's left of it—twists your way. An arm jerks upward, the nozzle pointing directly at you. A spray of chemicals hits you head-on. All you can do is stumble away, gasping and coughing. You blink, eyes filling with tears and skin burning as the blurry form of Roxy comes running to you.

But before she reaches you, everything goes dark.

GAME OVER

➤ TO START FROM THE BEGINNING, TURN TO PAGE 3.

➤ TO TRY THIS NIGHT AGAIN, TURN TO PAGE 168.

At the rate the Reagent is gaining, you're not going to make it to the top of the stairs in time. You can reach the bottom, though, so that will have to be enough.

"Roxy!" you cry. "Get ready!"

You can't see her from where you are, but if she's in position, your plan will work.

You hope.

At the bottom of the stairs you stop and turn. The Reagent is close behind, flying across the lobby floor as it gains on you. You take a deep breath and hold it, trying to stay steady. You wait as it gets closer . . . closer . . . until . . .

"Now, Roxy!"

You throw yourself out of the way as the Reagent bears down on you. At the top of the stairs, Roxy appears, pushing a huge crate, which she shoves down the stairs at your signal. It bumps and bangs as it tumbles down, but Roxy's aim is perfect; the crate hits the Reagent with a metallic *crunch*, sending bits and pieces of the bot flying. The bot—or what is left of it—comes to a stop at the edge of the Freddy fountain.

Roxy runs down the stairs, offering you a hand and helping you up. "Is it destroyed, Cassie?"

"I'm not sure."

You approach carefully. But by the time you reach the bot, you know your caution is unwarranted. What was once a Reagent is now in about a hundred different pieces, none of which is much of a threat anymore.

"We did it!" you cry.

"What a relief!" Roxy puts a hand on your shoulder.

You look up at her and smile. She returns your grin. As tempting as it is to remain with Roxy now that the Reagent is defeated, you've had enough of the Pizzaplex for a while. It's time to get out of here!

Roxy seems to sense that. "Come on, I'll walk you out."

Together, you go to the main entrance. When you try a door, it opens for you, letting in a blast of cool air that hints at dawn's arrival.

It's almost morning. Almost time for another day in the Pizzaplex. But you'll be long gone before the crowds arrive.

"Come play with us again," Roxy says, waving good-bye.

"Oh, don't worry," you say, stepping through the door and out of the Pizzaplex. "I will!"

Without the chemicals, the Reagent can't spray you. Lunging forward, you grab the plug on the bot's chemical tanks and pry it free. Immediately, a thick, viscous fluid begins to pour from the tanks, spreading across the floor beneath you. The Reagent tries to attack again, finally getting the nozzle pointed your way. You jump back, but nothing comes out of it. The Reagent tries for a few more seconds, but then, overcome by the effort, it goes limp and doesn't move again.

Roxy comes over. "Is it dead?"

You rub at your nose. The puddle of chemicals beneath you is still spreading, and it reeks. "I think so."

Roxy lets out a sigh of relief. "Thank goodness."

"I'll say." Then, you begin to cough. A strange taste spreads in your mouth, and your nose starts to sting.

"Are you okay, Cassie?" Roxy asks.

"Yeah, I . . ." Again, you cough, your throat beginning to burn. "I just think the . . . *cough* . . . something is . . ."

You step away from the broken Reagent, but the feeling persists, spreading until your chest is burning, too. Looking down at the puddle, you get a bad feeling. The chemicals . . .

"Roxy, I think I . . ." You gasp, unable to say anything else. Roxy comes toward you, but your head is beginning to swim, and your vision turns blurry. You fall to the ground, unable to move. There's a face staring at you . . . the face of the destroyed Reagent.

It's the last thing you see before the darkness overtakes you.

GAME OVER

➤ TO START FROM THE BEGINNING, TURN TO PAGE 3.

➤ TO TRY THIS NIGHT AGAIN, TURN TO PAGE 168.

Quickly, you reach into your bag and pull out the can of Sodaroni you found earlier. You know the pepperoni-flavored soft drink isn't very good for you; hopefully, it will be even worse for the Reagent! It hisses as you pull the tab open. You lean over the battered remains of the bot, dodging its weakly flailing limbs as you reach for the cover on its chemical tank. You flip it open and pour the soda in, emptying the whole can. Then you stand back.

For a moment, nothing happens. The Reagent continues to try to point its nozzles at you. Then, the arm freezes. There's a hissing sound, but not like the one when it sprayed the chemicals. Instead, this hiss comes from within the chemical tank. Suddenly, liquid begins to violently bubble out of the Reagent's tank, pouring over the robot and onto the floor. Anywhere it touches, the metal starts to corrode. You jump back as a horrible smell fills the air.

"What's happening?" cries Roxy.

You cover your nose. "I'm not sure. But I don't think it's good for the Reagent."

The robot starts to spasm and shake. The oozing, bubbling liquid is coming even faster now, reminding you of the vinegar-and-baking-soda volcanos you used to make in science class. Then, the Reagent gives off one last sad, metallic shriek and goes still.

You did it. The Reagent is destroyed.

Letting out a relieved sigh, you turn to Roxy. "It's dead."

"Thank goodness!" she exclaims. "Way to go, Cassie!"

"Now it's time to get out of here!" You start to turn away, but something catches your eye. A card sticking out from a compartment in the remains of the Reagent. You reach over and pull it out. It's an Executive Clearance key card. You decide to take it. After all, it might come in handy another night.

But for now, you've had enough of the Pizzaplex.

Roxy accompanies you to the front entrance of the Pizzaplex. When you try the door, it opens immediately; whatever locking protocol there was is now apparently gone with the

Reagent's demise. The cool night air hits you. It's almost morning.

"Don't stay away too long," says Roxy, sounding a little forlorn. "I'll miss you."

"Oh, don't worry," you reply. You smile at her. "I'll be back!"

Then you step out of the Pizzaplex, alive and well.

THE END

> **ADD THE EXECUTIVE CLEARANCE KEY CARD TO YOUR INVENTORY. NOW THAT YOU HAVE EXECUTIVE CLEARANCE KEY CARD BONUS ITEM, TURN TO PAGE 118 AND START OVER FROM NIGHT 4 FOR A NEW ADVENTURE.**

Working quickly, you fumble through your bag, pulling out the screwdriver you found. Below you, the Reagent is jerking and sparking, still determined to complete its mission despite being heavily damaged. You dodge a swinging appendage, stabbing out with the screwdriver. The metal tip connects with one of the circuit boards, snapping it free. The Reagent shudders but keeps moving. There's a burbling sound in its chemical tanks and you know you don't have long. You stab with the screwdriver again and again until the Reagent's innards are so smashed up it looks more like a pile of trash than the insides of a mechanical creature.

Finally, with one last spasm, the Reagent goes still.

"Is it . . . is it destroyed?" Roxy comes up beside you, still wary.

You take a deep breath and let it out. "I think so."

"Phew." Roxy smiles warmly at you. "That was close."

It sure was. Now . . . "Okay, what's the fastest way out of here?"

As tempting as it is to stay with Roxy now that the Reagent lies still, you've had enough of the Pizzaplex for a while.

"I know an exit in the back of the raceway," says Roxy. "Follow me."

She leads you to a door with a bright red EXIT sign above it. When you try it, it opens. The Reagent's programming may have kept the Pizzaplex in lockdown, but that's over now.

"You were very brave tonight," says Roxy, looking a little sad that you are leaving.

"So were you." You smile at the animatronic wolf. "Don't worry, Roxy. I'll be back soon!"

With that, you push the door open, taking a deep breath of the cool night air as you walk out of the Pizzaplex, alive.

Even badly damaged, the Reagent is still a threat. Its limbs flail, trying to take aim at you. Moving quickly, you dart forward and reach for the open hatch on the bot's chest, grabbing the wires and yanking.

An electric shock jolts through you. You cry out and stumble back, your skin burning where it touched the wires. Worse, pulling them out didn't seem to do anything. The Reagent shudders again, one of its nozzles flying up and pointing directly at you. You try to cry out, but the chemicals begin to spray, choking you before you can make a sound. You turn away and try to get to safety. But you only manage a few steps before your limbs begin to tremble. A moment later, they stop working altogether. The only thing you can do is cough and gasp as you fall to the raceway floor. There, you roll on your back, staring up at the shadowed ceiling above.

Tears fill your eyes. Beyond that blur, a familiar shape appears: Roxy.

But she's too late this time.

The last thing you hear is Roxy, calling your name, before the darkness descends.

GAME OVER

> TO START FROM THE BEGINNING, TURN TO PAGE 3.
> TO TRY THIS NIGHT AGAIN, TURN TO PAGE 168.

You're tired of trying to avoid the Reagent. It's time to deal with it, head-on. You look at Roxy's hands, the ones you upgraded with the new claws you found in Monty's greenroom. With those accessories, she might actually be a match for the Reagent.

You point at the claws. "Roxy, do you think you're up for confronting the Reagent if I lure it out?"

Roxy looks down at her hands. She flexes her fingers, the razor-sharp tips winking in the light. "Oh yeah. If you think it'll work, Cassie, I've got your back!"

You creep through the Pizzaplex, listening for any evidence of the bot. You're near the Prize Counter, which is where you saw it last. You swallow, nervous to be acting as bait, but you also know you don't have a choice. If you're going to deal with the Reagent, you need to lure it out into the open.

No point in being subtle, you think. "Hey!" Your voice sounds super loud in the deserted Pizzaplex, echoing a little. "Hey, bot! Are you looking for me? Here I am!"

At first, you think your efforts have come to nothing. Then, suddenly, you hear the sound of something getting closer. It's a sound you recognize all too well by now.

The Reagent appears, rushing at you. Turning, you run, bolting back across the Pizzaplex. But the Reagent is moving faster than you expected, closing in. You need to make it back to the mainstage, but if you don't move faster . . .

Fear gives you one last burst of energy, enough to carry you into the mainstage area. "Roxy, get ready!"

You're almost to the stage when you trip suddenly, sprawling across the floor. In a heartbeat, the Reagent is upon you, nozzles primed and ready.

A roar sounds above you as Roxy launches herself off the stage, landing between you and the Reagent. Her claws arc down and the nozzles go flying, sliced cleanly off the Reagent's arms. The bot flails, making an angry, screeching sound, but Roxy continues her attack, clawing at it again and again. You hear the sound of metal tearing as you get to your feet and back away, ready to run again if you need to. But Roxy's blows are relentless; within moments, she's made short work of the Reagent. It attempts to roll backward, then falls onto its side, shuddering once before going still.

You wait, but it doesn't move again. "You did it, Roxy! The Reagent is dead!"

Roxy sighs with relief. "Thank goodness." She flexes her claws again. "Or, actually, thank these babies. I think I'll keep them."

"Good idea," you say, feeling safe for the first time in a long time. "Now, I think it's time for me to get out of here."

Roxy looks a little sad but nods. "I'll walk you to the exit."

With Roxy at your side, you make your way to the front of the Pizzaplex. When you try the doors, they open easily, whatever locking protocol they had ended along with the Reagent.

"Thanks, Roxy," you say.

She smiles. "Come back soon, Cassie. I'll miss you."

Then you step outside the Pizzaplex into the cool night air. A dark figure outside the entrance turns as you exit.

It's Gregory. He gives you the biggest, most mischievous grin, then says: "So what game do you want to play tomorrow night?"

THE END

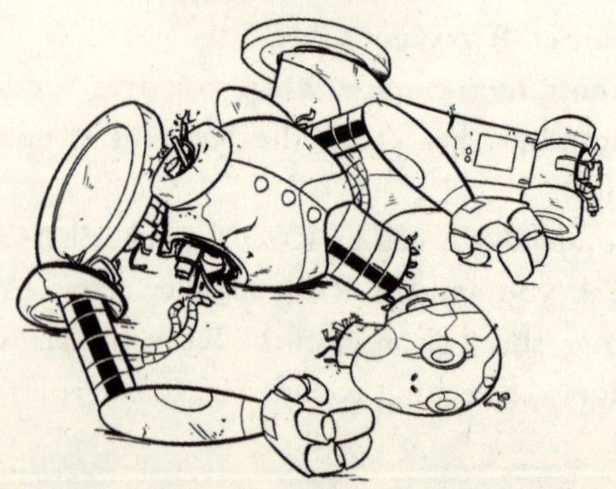

ABOUT THE AUTHORS

SCOTT CAWTHON is the author of the bestselling video game series *Five Nights at Freddy's*, and while he is a game designer by trade, he is first and foremost a storyteller at heart. He is a graduate of the Art Institute of Houston and lives in Texas with his family.

LYNDSAY ELY is the author of *Gunslinger Girl*, a YA genre-bent dystopian Western that was published in 2018, as well as the *Overwatch* novel *Deadlock Rebels* and short story "Luck of the Draw." She spent her teenage years wanting to be a comic book artist, but, as it turned out, she couldn't draw very well, so she began writing instead. She is a geek and a foodie, and has never met an antique shop or flea market she didn't like. Boston is the place she currently calls home, though she wouldn't mind giving Paris a try someday.

NOTES